Witch of the Silver Locust

DAWN OF THE BLOOD WITCH BOOK 3

Maria DeVivo

Witch of the
Silver Locust

DAWN OF THE BLOOD WITCH BOOK 3

Maria DeVivo

4 Horsemen
Publications, Inc.

Witch of the Silver Locust
Dawn of the Blood Witch Book 3
Copyright © 2023 Maria DeVivo. All rights reserved.

4 Horsemen
Publications, Inc.

4 Horsemen Publications, Inc.
1497 Main St. Suite 169
Dunedin, FL 34698
4horsemenpublications.com
info@4horsemenpublications.com

Cover by J. Kotick
Typeset by S. Wilder
Editor Laura Mita

Library of Congress Control Number: 2022943394

Paperback ISBN-13: 979-8-8232-0015-8
Hardcover ISBN-13: 978-1-64450-773-5
Audiobook ISBN-13: 979-8-8232-0013-4
Ebook ISBN-13: 979-8-8232-0014-1

Dedication:

For Joe – You are *my* conduit—the one who open the pathways for me to make all things possible. Thank you for everything and always.

For Alex – For all your enthusiasm, all your help, all your support, and all your time. You have always been, and always will be very special to me. I'm thankful for the friendship we have now, even though you're still 12 in my eyes.

For Morgan – It's always for you, and always will be for you … just maybe when you're much older.

Table of Contents

Every tale has a beginning. The third book in the Dawn of the Blood Witch Saga tells the origin story of the mysterious and powerful witch Trond, the Witch of the Silver Locust. Split into three separate timelines, the Silver Locust encounters friends and foes, both new and old, as he tries to open the gateway to the old ones and bring about the witch utopia of New Eden on Earth.

Inspired by true events, he will have to endure an exorcism, the Church of Satan, and the Son of Sam if he wishes to fulfill his destiny.

Part 1

Chapter One

In the Time of Darkness
In the Age of Ice
Summertime, 760 AD
Caverns in the Far North
Night of the Full Moon

The fires burned low inside the gray abode, yet the shadows from the full moon peeking her rays into the mouth of the cave cast eerie shadows against the rocky walls. Jagged faces and distorted bodies took shape and flickered and flitted across the rocks. For a split second, I was filled with wistful longing and hope that struck me deep in my heart. Had the spirits come home to me? I breathed in and held my breath for a few seconds in wild anticipation, and like an optimistic little boy, I quietly whispered, "Please come home. Please come home. Please come…" But then a breeze blew in, and the shadow figures disappeared and shifted into something different. My heart sank, and I was once again overcome with that never-ending sense of misery and anguish.

I sighed heavily with despair and made my way to my altar in the corner of the cave. It was situated deep enough so that it was somewhat hidden from the wandering traveler, nosey neighbor, or some other intruder to our home. It appeared to be an abandoned hearth or cooking station. The light from the fires at the front of the cavern scarcely reached it, so it remained tucked away and secret. But it was no secret. Not to me at least. That altar was my whole world now. It represented everything I had lost, everything that was stolen from me, and everything I was determined to reclaim and bring back into existence—for if Blodwyn could do it, I would do it, too.

My sister Blodwyn was the greatest witch I had ever known. Her power and strength were known far and wide throughout the villages, even reaching the outer skirts of the more nomadic lands. Our mother had been the town healer, a Heksa in her own right, but Blodwyn far surpassed Mother's talents and abilities. All I knew of my mother was from the stories passed down to me. She had died while bringing me into this world, and when that day had come, Blodwyn, seventeen years my senior, swooped me from between our mother's legs, washed me off, and called me hers from the moment of my first breath. Mother had given me a name before I was born, but Blodwyn had nicknamed me Ruz—for I had been born of a Blodheksa and my birthing blood had stained my silver baby hair to bright pink. Ruz Solvven. *Pink Silver*. She affectionately teased me often about that.

From the moment I could understand words, Blodwyn had established that she was my caretaker, my protector, my mentor, my teacher, and my sister, but I was commanded to never confuse that with the title of "mother." As a child, though, hearing the other children in our village speak the word "modir" to *their* caretakers was a little jarring. That was not a word in my physical reality. My modir was an entity—a non-corporeal object, a word spoken on the wind. Once, many years ago when I was three years old, I called Blodwyn "modir" just to see her reaction. I was curious if she would find it endearing and embrace the title like snapping into a new way of thinking. However, it was the opposite. She turned on me with great fury and struck me across the face. "Modir is gone, Ruz!" she had screamed. "Modir was taken away! But I will fix that. Mark my words. I swear it by the sky, and the moon, and the sun, and the stars, and the fixed iced earth, and the great beyond! I will slice open the sky and pull her back through the circle." She raised her hand to the sky and waved

4

it in an arching gesture. "For she is the Blodheksa, the Blood Witch who will open the gateway." She closed her fist and struck her chest. "And I am the Blodsøster, the Blood Sister who will aid the Blodheksa in her mission." She pointed her forefinger and jabbed it into the crook of my shoulder. "And you are the Blodbrødre, the Blood Brother who will fight by my side for eternity in the new world. This is how it must be."

That was the first time I saw her eyes change color. They flashed gray, to gold, to green, to white. At first, I thought it was my imagination or my head still ringing from the open-handed smack she had walloped me with. But no. Her eyes changed. It was as clear as day and forever burned in my memory. And it was at that very moment, at three years of age, that I understood—I understood that we were different from other families in our village, different from other people in this world.

And that's how it was—our mother was gone, hidden somewhere in the shadows, somewhere in the great void between this life and the next. Blodwyn always preached about Mother's eventual return. Thoughts of Mother's resurrection consumed her day and night. I remember watching Blodwyn agonize over her altar, conjuring dark magics, mixing deadly potions, and making just the right combinations to will the Blodheksa back into form.

And if she was successful, then I shall be, too...

I knelt in front of the altar, raised my arms above my head, and began the prayer I had recited since the night Blodwyn died. It was a chant, really, a dirge of lamentation. A song of need and want and desire to raise not just her soul, but her body as well, from the great beyond. But I felt empty. Despondent. Useless...

"Trond?" a soft voice called from the mouth of the cave. "Trond? Are you here?"

Aizel, my companion, had returned from the outer village. I stood up and quickly shuffled closer to the fires, but not fast enough for her to catch me in the act. She put her hand on one hip and bounced impatiently on one leg. "That was fast," I muttered.

Her mouth made a condescending "tsk" sound that echoed throughout the cave, and as she fully entered, she slid the strap of her pack down one shoulder, emptying the contents onto the ground. Her tools clanked when they hit the stones, and she shook the pack with force to expel the pieces of blood-soaked cloth.

"Fast enough. It was Brigitta's third child, so…" Her voice trailed as she bent over to pick up the scraps of fabric. "Here." She extended her arm to hand them to me. "Put these on the altar with the others from the other day. Brigitta and Helga are cousins so their birthing blood could…"

"Did the mother and child survive?" I asked.

Aizel rolled her eyes and sighed. "Of all the years. Of all the babies I've delivered. You're seriously asking this of me now? How many children have died on my watch? Do you think I would give you the blood of the dead? Do I not know how this is to be?"

I lowered my head in shame. "I'm sorry…"

"I know what you were doing, Trond," she scolded. "I'm not stupid. And I've told you, it might not be time yet. We must have all the proper instruments in place. We must have the stars aligned just so. We must be patient…"

Aizel's words struck me deep and ignited a flame in my stomach. "Patient?" I screamed. "Patient? How much more patience do we need to have before we give up?" My eyes filled with tears, and I turned my head from her so that she couldn't see my anger and sadness getting the best of me.

She placed a hand on my shoulder in comfort. "I want Blodwyn back as much as you do, Trond. She wasn't just yours. She was mine, as well. She was everything to me, too."

I turned back to look at her, and her soft blue eyes were also rimmed with tears. Aizel had been Blodwyn's best friend, her confidante, her rock. They had been inseparable and had shared a love like no other. I know it pained her, too, that we had been unsuccessful in resurrecting Blodwyn, but all these years of futile attempts and constant excuses left my heart soured to her. I knew first-hand what Blodwyn could do. I witnessed the enormous power she wielded, and I wanted that power for myself, if for anything but to bring her back.

Aizel exhaled. Her sigh bounced off the rock wall and pierced my eardrums with a timbre that bore utter disgust. "There isn't a book about this. We have no instructions on how to proceed. We need to continue exploring all the possibilities by our mere intuition. Blodwyn left no other guidance than that," she pleaded with me as if reading my mind.

Startled, I paused. Aizel and I had made a promise long ago that we would never enter each other's minds unless it was an emergency. I tapped my forefinger to the side of my temple. "Get out of there," I admonished calmly.

My tone must have frightened her, for she took a step back and a look of concern briefly darkened her face. "Think what you will," she began trying to brush off my threat, "but she charged me with watching over you."

"And when will that end, Aizel? I'm no longer a boy."

She grazed her eyes over my figure from my feet to my head. "No, Trond. You haven't been a boy for quite some time."

"And yet, here I am. The body and countenance of a man of two hundred forty moon cycles. Yet that is not the truth. My time on this iced earth far surpasses that. And you... the face and body of a woman of childbearing age. Instead of delivering all those children, they should be falling out from between your legs by now. But how long and how old are we? The gift given to us by Blodwyn left us ageless on the outside, but are your insides rotted? You cannot be the Blodheksa if you can't produce the twins! It has been months since you laid with me. You are too consumed with that book you're writing, and those babies you're dragging into the world. Why haven't you let me touch you? Why haven't you allowed me inside of you? Is your womb as desolate a cave as the place we...?"

Aizel struck me across the face, and I quickly reached my hand up to my cheek to ease the sting. "Enough!" she yelled, silencing my tirade, and I was suddenly transported back to the moment when Blodwyn hit me. For the first time in a long time, I felt small, and weak, and useless. Like a child.

"Aizel, I..." I stammered, but she quickly cut me off.

7

"Enough, Trond." Her voice was soft again, pleading me with, yet trying to find its own sense of rationale. "We are not just heksas, we are the Aevir, the eternal ones. A gift given to us by Blodwyn. And we will remain Aevir until the task at hand is complete, until our roles are fulfilled." She lowered her head, and her mass of red curls tumbled and hung heavy on the floor. "I know I'm not the Blodheksa," she said in a sad whisper. "I wanted to be. I prayed to be. I longed to be. But I know I'm not. Our restless nights together have brought forth no child let alone the Blood Sister and Blood Brother."

"So, what are you?" I spat at her with repulsion. "Was all this a lie?"

"No, Trond. Not lies. Just because we have yet to unravel the secrets of it all doesn't mean we were lied to." She put her hand on my shoulder again and ran her fingers down the length of my arm until our hands met in an interlocking grasp. "What is the goal of our way?" she asked, prompting me to recite the tenants of our faith.

"The Blodheksa will bring forth the Blodbrødre and the Blodsøster."

"And who is the Blodheksa?" she asked.

"The most powerful witch in the world."

"And who are the Blood Brother and the Blood Sister?" she urged me on.

"Her children who are the fixed points. They will be the vessels of her power and assist her in her goal," I parroted back the words that had been ingrained in me from birth.

She smiled at my response. "And what is their goal?"

"To open up the realms so the old ones can reign again."

She squeezed my hand tightly, and her eyes lit up with pride at my response. "Lest not forget that. That is our core. Everything we do, we do with that in mind. You know I want Blodwyn back just as much as you do, but we can't let our efforts for her rebirth blind us in the efforts of our main objective. Do you understand me, Trond?"

I nodded. Begrudgingly. "And that's why you've taken to writing it all down?"

"Yes. The records. All of it. I dreamt of six books, so six I must write. One alone will take a lifetime. The dream told me we need to have a living record of our history. And who would write it all down? If not me, then who?"

Anger swelled again inside me. I knew Aizel was trying to snap me out of my lowly state and bring my focus and attention back to what we've always strived to accomplish, but something inside me was unsettled. It felt to me as if she was forgetting Blodwyn. As if she was forgetting the supreme nature of her power. We couldn't achieve our goal of a new world without Blodwyn; I knew that for a fact. Blodwyn was the key. And even though I'd lost count of the moon cycles that had passed since she died, I knew I could never give up on bringing her back.

I reached out, grabbed Aizel by the shoulders, and pulled her to me. I bent down slightly and pressed my lips to hers, my tongue dancing wildly in and out. Her mouth was warm and inviting, and I began to stir between my legs at the very taste of her sweetness. For a moment, I felt her swoon against my hold and let herself ease into my passionate kiss, but after a while, she stopped and pulled away. "No," she said. "We can't."

"Why?" I asked as my forehead crinkled in confusion.

"We shouldn't."

"It's nothing we haven't done before!" I pleaded as the ache in my loins throbbed.

"I know," she said in a muffled voice. "It's just that..."

I gave her a little shove away from my space and turned my back to her.

We were silent in the cave for some time. I kept my back to her in defiance, and she proceeded to pick up the tools from the ground and put them back in her pack. After a few minutes, she mumbled something about it being too warm out for a second fire and extinguished one of them. The hissing noise echoed, and it grated on my every nerve.

"We're going to have to leave here, you know," she eventually said.

Sharply, I whipped my head around in her direction. "Whatever are you talking about? This is our home. This has always been our home. We're not going anywhere."

"The people in the villages are starting to talk. They've always talked, but this time it's louder."

I sighed noisily. I always hated when she didn't get straight to the point. "What are you saying?" I huffed with an agitated tone.

"We're the same, Trond. I delivered Brigitta's baby tonight, but I also delivered Brigitta, and I delivered Brigitta's mother, Alsin. Alsin is but forty years old, and by that measure, I should be sixty. At the least."

"And your point is?"

"My point is, the time is coming soon to where all those who knew us from yesteryear will be gone, and the new blood will begin to question. They will investigate and poke and prod, and before you know it, we'll be led to the slaughter for being otherworldly."

"But we *are* otherworldly," I said flatly.

Aizel huffed an exasperated sigh. "You're not understanding."

"Oh, I understand just fine. I hear what you're saying. You think we're going to be persecuted by the people for being different. For knowing things and doing things they can't understand to know or do."

"I don't think. I know."

"And you want to leave our cave? Blodwyn's cave? The place where she died and where her ashes remain! Are you suggesting we erase ourselves? Erase our names? Erase Blodwyn?"

"Trond! I'm not saying I *want* to leave! I'm saying we're going to *have* to leave. Eventually. Sooner than later. It's something we need to plan for."

I raised my hand to silence her, and she muffled a groan in her throat. "Hey," she cried out as I began to walk to the back of the cave, "you're not allowed to do that!"

"Well, stay out of my head next time!" I fired back.

She grumbled some more, but as I advanced to my personal area, her voice became nothing more than a garbled din.

No sooner had I been out of earshot, there was a rustling from outside the cave walls and a heavyweight presented itself on my chest. My senses picked up on it immediately. A darkness blanketed the cave, and I set myself at a sprinter's pace to reach Aizel where I had left her. Regardless of any squabble between us, she was still first and foremost mine—to love, and serve, and protect.

As quickly as I could, I bounded by her side. She was frozen in place with a look of confusion and fear plastered on her countenance. Instinctively, I wrapped my arm around her shoulders and pulled her closer to me in a defensive stance. Her gaze never wavered, and she continued to stare at the scene before us at the entrance of our cave.

"Please," the black-haired man begged as he laid the body of the young girl onto the ground. "Please help her. You are the one named Aizel Olz. The midwife. But the people say you are a great and knowledgeable heksa. You are the only one who can help my sweet girl. Please. I have no one else to turn to," the man wept. Heaving sobs churned from the center of his barrel chest.

I brought Aizel tighter into me as she looked up into my eyes. They flashed from soft blue, to green, to gray. Eyes that spoke of both uncertainty and fear. "What is wrong with your daughter, sir?" she asked, her voice quivering with each word.

The man stood up and took a step back, observing the girl on the floor. She appeared lifeless. Her knees curled to her chest and her long black hair blanketed the granite floor. "She's gone," he cried.

"Oh," Aizel managed to say. "I'm so sorry, but if your daughter has passed, I can't help you."

Suddenly, the girl shifted—a sharp, quick movement that was both unanticipated and unnatural. Aizel's body tensed up against me and she squeaked.

"No!" the man wailed. "Something has taken over her! Please. I beg you. You must get it out!"

Chapter Two

In the Time of Darkness
In the Age of Ice
Summertime, 760 AD
Caverns in the Far North
Night of the Full Moon

The black-haired girl on the floor shifted slightly. Her leg jutted straight out from under her curled position, then seemed to lock back in place. But the movements were quick and jerky and not the natural motion and flow that the human body usually glides around with. Aizel's eyes went wide, and she squeezed the back of my leg with her right hand. Her feeling of alarm quickly spread to me as my legs seemed to lock in place and my gaze trained on the girl at our feet.

"Where are you from, sir?" Aizel asked after some time.

"I am Sten. From the outer village."

Aizel's grip on the back of my leg tightened. What she had spoken of earlier appeared to be true. Our reputations had extended out to the nomadic lands—beyond the interior villages, beyond the newer structures that were being built with wood, and beyond the fortification walls. The nomadic lands were mostly a mystery to the people in the inner compound. Not many had wanted to venture off and away from the comfort and protection of their modest caves and huts. Most never

returned if they did—often dying from the wildlife or starvation or from finding a mate and roaming with the pack.

"This is Runa, my daughter," Sten's voice grew desperate. "Please. I have come such a long way. Please help us."

Aizel relaxed her grip on me and breathed heavily. I had no way of telling what was going through her mind at that moment. My first instinct was to send them away, tell him to drag his daughter up from the ground, leave and never look for us again. We had been distrusting of outsiders for as long as I could remember, and this was no different. But there was something in Aizel's demeanor that told me otherwise. She moved cautiously to the girl and knelt beside her. Runa's long black hair was strewn over the rocks and covered her face. Aizel gathered the ebony mass into one hand and swept it aside to examine her. The girl was pale—much paler than the normal tones of someone from the outer village. She was still and death-like in appearance. Had her body not jolted in my presence earlier, I would have mistaken her for dead. She also had a tiny build—small in stature with her cheek bones jutting out sharply from the side of her face. When Sten had first dropped her to the ground, I assumed she was a girl of no more than twelve, but as Aizel revealed Runa's countenance, it was obvious she was much older.

"Is she sick?" Aizel asked as she began her examination.

"Yes!" Sten cried out. "That's what I've been trying to tell you."

Aizel waved her hand dismissively. "No, I mean is she ill? Unwell? Does she have a cough? Was she experiencing pain in her head? Was she running a fever?"

Sten shook his head furiously. "No! No! Nothing like that."

"Was she attacked by an animal? Bitten? A spider, maybe? A snake? Venom, poison?"

"No! Runa is a good girl. She listens. She takes care of me. She makes the fire. She cooks the food. She mends the clothes. She stakes the tents. She knows what to eat and what to stay away from. She knows the land from which she was born."

Aizel ran her hand down Runa's neck and made gentle pressing motions as if searching for something. She hummed a little when everything seemed to be in order, straightened out Runa's curled-up legs and began pressing gently on her abdomen. "Hmmm," she seemed to sing. "Is she with child?"

Sten's eyes widened. His thick black eyebrows disappeared under his shaggy hair. "With... with child?" he stammered. "No. Nothing like that. She does not have a mate. There's... there is no one." A shock of pink bloomed on his pale cheeks.

Aizel glared at me, and I gave her a knowing look. We both knew the father's denial meant absolutely nothing. But after pressing some more on her abdomen and squeezing her breasts for the tell-tale signs of life swelling inside her, Aizel determined that Runa was in fact not pregnant.

Yet, throughout Aizel's initial examination, Runa remained in a comatose state. Aside from the twitches and jolts her body made when they first arrived, she had not moved again, nor had she opened her eyes. "Sir, can you tell me what happened? Can you tell me why you believe there is something inside your daughter? Does she... have the sight?"

Sten knelt beside Aizel and looked over his shoulder as if to insure we were alone. He began in a hushed voice, and his words came out feverishly, as if he needed to rush through the story so as to not be heard or discovered by someone, or something.

"I believe she can commune with the otherworld. Not often, but I have seen her go into a... a... a *trance*. Ever since she was a little girl. We ignored it. Thought it might have been an affliction in her brain."

Aizel hummed some more. "What exactly happened that led up to her sickness—to her being like this?"

"I can't say when it happened, but about fourteen moon nights ago, Runa went for a walk."

"By herself?" Aizel asked.

Sten nodded. "A few hours after she had returned, she took ill."

Aizel rested her backside on her heels and motioned for me to join them, but I already knew. She and I had worked side by side for so many years that we no longer had to signal into each other's minds the images of our needs. We worked so flawlessly in tandem that I already knew she wanted me to give the girl another look. As I eased myself next to Aizel,

I immediately reached for Runa's arm, rolled up her long sleeve, and began carefully inspecting every inch of her skin. She was limp, like dead weight. I was able to do my own poking and prodding and nary a single stir came from the girl. It was eerie enough a feeling for me to place my hand over her nose to determine if she still breathed. When the soft air came from her nostrils, I sighed and continued my inspection. I did not speak or interject myself into the conversation. I just listened and observed.

"What do you mean she took ill?" Aizel asked.

"She said she felt sick in her stomach."

"Are you sure she wasn't bitten by something?"

"Yes. Yes. Her mother asked if she had eaten something in the woods, or if something struck her, or stung her, to which she replied 'no, no, no.' She's grown up on the lands. At seventeen years old, I think I'm inclined to believe my daughter. Besides, she didn't present with the usual poisoning symptoms."

Aizel ignored his fatherly justification. "What happened next?"

"There was some meat leftover from the hunt that day. Gyda cooked some up, fed it to Runa, and she appeared to feel better."

"Gyda?"

"Runa's mother," Sten gushed, and tears poured down his face. "My sweet, sweet wife."

Aizel put her hand on his knee. "Please. Go on." She coaxed.

Sten inhaled deeply and exhaled with a "whooo," as if to steady his breathing and clear his thoughts back into focus. "Everything was fine from there. Runa was a little tired and sluggish, but what teenage girl doesn't get that way during her moon time?" He tried to let out a little chuckle. "Then one night, she awoke screaming from a dream. Gyda and I rushed to her tent, and she was soaking wet from fright. She was saying something about a pair of hands pulling her mouth open, and she couldn't move or fight against them. I thought for sure someone in the camp had tried to attack her, but she insisted they weren't the hands of man. She said they didn't *feel* like the hands of man. Gyda and I calmed her down from her nightmare, and she went back to sleep."

"It didn't end there, did it?"

Sten slowly shook his head. "Every night after that was the same. Screaming from the nightmares. By the third nightfall, Gyda decided to sleep in her tent so she would be able to calm her down right away. But then. The other morning…" Sten's voice trailed, and his breath hitched in his throat. I picked up Runa's other arm to examine it and noticed deep brown flecks under her fingernails. I turned my head to Aizel to get her attention, but she was fixated on poor, sobbing Sten.

"She killed her," I finally said. "She killed your wife."

At the sound of my voice, Runa's body began to convulse. The three of us jumped up, startled.

"No!" Sten cried. "Not again! Hold her down!" He shouted.

Aizel leapt on top and straddled Runa's upper body while Sten bent forward and secured her legs. The girl thrashed and jerked with such brute force it was no wonder she didn't crack her head wide open on the rock floor of the cave. And all the while, I stood by and watched the scene unfold before me. It was mesmerizing—the unnatural shaking of her body, the growling sounds gurgling from the base of her throat, her hair dancing wildly about her face.

And then, Runa finally opened her eyes and stared at me. They were like two black gems gleaming in the moonlight—magical and awe-inspiring. When I gazed back, my heart was set aflame, and I was consumed in their charm and power. Her eyes held me locked in place, swaying in time with the rhythm of her spasm. Her eyes took me far away—to another time fresh beyond my comprehension of existence, to another place with dancing trees in a forest of metal, and an opening in the sky, glittering on the edge of the cosmos. Her eyes took me through that void, and I saw the world that we had so longed to create. And I was there, and Aizel was there, and Blodwyn was there, and we were accompanied by a line of heksas that spanned through time and space. Hundreds upon hundreds of years. And I saw the old ones lumbering through the vast terrain. Their gnarled bodies outstretched for miles against the red horizon, and the line of heksas bowing in supplication to their splendor and glory. It was magnificent. I wanted to stay in that vision forever—stay trapped in Runa's eyes until the end of time.

"Trond! Trond!" Aizel's screams broke into my mind. But it was more than just her screaming. She had slashed her way through my consciousness with all her force and energy like a hot poker searing the flesh of a downed elk. "Help me!" she screamed again, and that time I snapped back into the present. "Get behind her! Lift her up!"

Runa's spasms had ceased, and she was limp and still once again, but a small puddle of her blood had formed by her head as I had suspected it would. Swiftly, I made my way over to her and lifted her shoulders, hoisting her to a semi-standing position. Sten came up next to me, propped one underside of her arm onto his shoulder, and I slithered over to mimic his actions on her other side.

"Take her to the back where the supplies are," Aizel instructed. "Place her at the wooden chair in the middle of the room."

"Not in my space?" I questioned. My tone of voice must have given Aizel cause for concern for she raised her eyebrows inquisitively at me.

"Nooooo," she drawled. "I think the storage alcove is more appropriate." She looked to Sten. "Once she's awake, I'll be able to get a clearer understanding of what's going on with your daughter. I have my suspicions but will not make a final judgment until I can speak to her."

Sten nodded tersely and we dragged Runa's wilted body to the back of the cave, her feet trailing behind her. Once there, we sat her upright in the chair as Aizel had instructed. She came up right behind us and wrapped a strong knotted rope around her to secure her in place.

"Is… is that necessary?" Sten asked.

"Consider it a precaution," she responded. "Here." She reached into one of the pockets of her apron and handed Sten a small satchel. "Go into the village. Daybreak will be upon us soon. Find a woman called Hilde. Tell her you need a pack for Aizel. She'll know exactly what you're talking about. Give her this and get back here as soon as you can."

Reluctantly, Sten took the pouch, nodded, and exited the cave.

"We have all the supplies at the altar," I said after Sten was out of sight.

"I know. I know. I needed him out of here. His presence isn't helping much, especially if he's going to question every move I make."

"You know what it is, don't you?" It was more of a statement than a question.

Aizel nodded. "I suspect."

I looked to Runa. Her head slumped forward in her seated position, and her black wavy hair touched the cold stone floor. Her breaths were coming in labored pants, and her chest heaved up and down frantically. I wanted to see her face — her sullen white face with her sharp cheekbones protruding from the sides like wings. I wanted to gaze into her mystical black eyes and be transported back to that place in my mind where the air was acrid, and the old ones ran free. I wanted to cup her small breasts in both my hands, spread her legs and...

"Stop it!" Aizel commanded, swatting me on the arm.

"What?" I implored. "What did I do?"

"You know exactly what you did. You declared to me before you were no longer a little boy, so stop thinking like one." She circled Runa with a close and meticulous eye.

"We promised, Aizel!" I exclaimed. "How many times has it been, tonight alone, that you've invaded my head?"

"Oh, stop it! Get over it. This is more serious than those words we proclaimed. Don't let yourself be fooled by this one." Aizel stopped behind Runa and hovered her hands above her head. Runa's breathing became more labored, more frantic, as Aizel's fingers tightened and arched and bobbed up and down above her. Soon, Aizel's eyes fluttered to the back of her head. I'd seen her do this before. She called it fishing.

"Did Runa actually kill her mother? How could this small-framed child carry out such an arduous task?"

"She didn't," Aizel said, swaying side to side. "It was something else." She hummed a little and continued to rock back and forth. The air in the room grew heavy with the metallic scent of dried blood like after a kill. When the animal's throat is slit and the blood spills onto the granite and splatters against the walls, and the smell takes over—that smell of death hovering over the firepit of life for that one moment before it snuffs it out. The energy grew. The depth of it, the breadth of it nearly suffocated me. Runa's breathing settled, and when Aizel released her hold on the girl, her upper body shot up at attention, her dark eyes opened wide, and she smiled from ear to ear.

Aizel strolled around to face her. "This one has a name. Don't you draugr?" she said in a sing-song voice.

Runa gave a small chuckle and eyed Aizel intently.

"How do you know? How can you be sure?" I asked, but even to my own ears, I sounded like a desperate little boy.

"It told me," Aizel responded, never breaking eye contact with the girl.

"And Runa?"

"Her father was right. Runa is gone. The demon is in her place now. Isn't that right draugr?"

Runa huffed. Or rather, the draugr huffed.

"So, when do we begin?" I asked. This wouldn't be the first draugr we dispatched, nor did I suspect it would be our last. Aizel had been long acquainted with the art of expulsion, and there was no other heksa I had known to lead the ritual as neatly and as efficiently as she.

She moved toward me, her back to the girl, and placed her hand on my shoulder. "We don't," she said in a hushed voice.

I pulled back in surprise. "What do you mean, we don't?"

"This is a draugr unlike any I've seen. When I transferred myself into the girl's mind, I saw terrible things. Monstrous things. If we try to expel it, there's no guarantee that we would be safe or even survive the expulsion for that matter."

Were the terrible things *she* saw just the beautiful things the demon showed *me*? How could the both of us bear witness to two vastly different scenarios?

"Safe? I saw it too, Aizel. This might be the answer we're looking for."

She grabbed the top of my shoulder. "Answer to what? Bringing Blodwyn back? Creating our new realm? If that's the case, you're forgetting a very important detail, Trond. The

Blodbrødre and Blodsøster. If we don't have them, we can't even think about the ritual."

"I don't know," I said, trying my best to convince her. "I feel like she is the key to all of this. A gift. A sign. What are the chances that this...?"

"Stop. I'm telling you true. This is not an answer to any of our questions." Aizel let go of me and walked to the opening of the room.

I turned to face her. "How can you be so sure, though?" I pleaded. "You haven't even given..."

"I don't have to. When I pulled out its name, that was all I needed. This is not something we want to get involved in, I promise you that."

"And what is its name?"

Aizel paused, glanced over at Runa behind me, then looked directly in my eyes. "Not one you would like to know."

"What about the girl? What happens if we let the draugr remain?"

"Stop asking questions you know the answer to. The draugr will consume the girl and eventually go back to whence it came. It's just a matter of time. Until then, we are to have no interaction or contact with it. Do you hear me, Trond? Do not engage it, entertain it, or fall prey to its many tricks. Tell me you understand. Promise me."

I nodded, and she walked away.

I turned to look back at Runa. Runa. The young woman with the waiflike build and jaggedly beautiful face. Runa of the blackest eyes that held the mysteries of the universe. And I wanted to dive into them. Drive myself into her. For her beauty and mystique were too enchanting to ignore. It was too coincidental that she would fall at my feet in my darkest moment of despair. She was the key. I knew it. She had to be.

But I trusted Aizel. I trusted her wisdom and knowledge. And if she had reservations about this, I needed to trust that as well.

Suddenly, Runa stirred. She moved against her restraints, scraping the legs of the chair slightly across the granite floor. She hummed and mumbled something inaudible at first, but I adjusted my preternatural hearing and homed in on the sound, and what she was saying, and the word that left her barely opened lips.

No. Not a word, but a name.

A name that groaned from the depths of her chest.

"Ruz."

Chapter Three

In the Time of Darkness
In the Age of Ice
Summertime, 760 AD
Caverns in the Far North
Night of the Waning Gibbous Moon

Three moon tides had passed, and Runa remained in our care. A subject? A prisoner? I could not truly tell the difference. Sten had returned to the cave that first night with the supplies Aizel told him to procure—supplies that were just a diversion so that she could make her final judgment on what was to be done with the girl. Aizel told Sten to set up camp in our village and wait for us to call for him. He knew she was well respected and that our people would take care of him if need be, so he left our cave to go into town and patiently waited until his child was delivered from the evil that took hold of her *hugr* and *fylgja*—in essence, her soul.

Sten was obedient and did as he was told—partly because he was a doting father who wanted to see his daughter healed, and partly, because at his core, he was a weak man who fell easily under Aizel's spell. She promised him she would do whatever she could to help Runa, and if that meant Sten had to run into a pack of snarling wolves, he would have complied. But I knew the truth. There was no intention of expelling the

22

draugr from the girl. Aizel was stalling for time as the demon inside Runa slowly festered and consumed her bit by bit.

And as the days passed, I purposefully and consciously locked my mind like a steal cage against Aizel so she couldn't go digging around. I hadn't told her what I had heard Runa say—how she had called out the sacred nickname my sister had bestowed upon me, for I knew she would have forbidden me to even go near the girl after that. Nevertheless, I was intrigued. How would she have known that name unless by some divine intervention? I was certainly convinced that this was more than just the average possession we were used to dealing with, and I was determined to find out more. What was this demon, and why had it made itself known to me the night of the full moon, and more specifically during a time of my great despondency?

So, without Aizel's knowledge of my actions, I stole away into the storage alcove where Runa had been tied up for the last three nights in hopes of getting as much information from the creature as I could. I brought my canteen of water under the assumption that maybe a drink would satisfy it and give it reason to open up. When I reached the room, the air was thick with an unnatural heat and a steamy sheen blanketed the space around us, much like the steam from the hot springs a bit south of us.

I stood in the opening and watched as Runa's slumped body breathed in and out with those frenzied pants. Her head tilted to one side as if the weight of her long, silky black hair was pulling her down in her slumber. She looked peaceful, even with her chest heaving up and down as frantically as it was. I wondered what type of frenetic dream she must be having. Was she running in a field? Were the wolves chasing her? Was a hoard of marauders ravaging her fragile body?

I dipped my foot gingerly across the imaginary threshold of the room, and suddenly she stopped, shot up, and opened her eyes wide. "All three," she cooed with a smirk.

I froze for a moment, surprised by her abrupt actions, then continued my way inside.

Runa smiled wide, and the evidence of the draugr's hold on her was blatantly clear. The soft pink tissue of her gums was coated with a dark black substance giving her mouth the appearance of a gaping void.

A void to swallow me whole and transport me to another dimension...

"You would like that, wouldn't you?" she blurted.

"You know I'm not afraid of you, right?" I said. "I've seen the likes of you before."

She giggled. "Oh, have you?" she responded. Her voice was low and gravelly, and it echoed in the cave as if there were more than one being speaking simultaneously. I couldn't tell if it was the acoustics or if she actually represented the power of the many. And the voice, that guttural, grinding tone was so familiar to me, yet I could not place where I'd heard it before.

I approached her in the chair and held my canteen to her face. She eyed me coolly. "No," she said. "It would just prolong the process."

"Oh? And what process is this you speak of?"

"I know your plans. The girl is gone. There's no use in saving her now."

I pursed my lips together and nodded. "True. True." I agreed. "But that doesn't mean you still can't serve a purpose for us."

The draugr laughed aloud. Its voice pierced the inside of my eardrums so sharply that I winced.

"Untie me, and I'll show you what purpose I can serve," she said with a sly hint of seduction.

I looked down upon her and scoffed. Up close I could see the demon had begun to transform her. Runa's visage had begun to crack. The pale skin of her once soft face had turned gray, and the dark green veins from beneath her skin pressed up close to the surface and pulsated as if they were their own living, breathing entities. Her cheeks had further sunken in, giving the sharp angles of her face an even more inhuman appearance. She grazed her thick black tongue across the surface of her dry lips. "I won't bite," she cooed.

I huffed and took a step back. "Do you think that's what it would take to tempt me? I told you, I've done this before.

You're not the first draugr to grace this cavern. Do you even know how old I am?"

"Do you even know how old *I* am?" she shot back.

I knelt next to her and decided to seize the opportunity. Demons are all-knowing, or at least they think they are. And they like to talk, mainly about themselves and their powers. And it's often their narcissism that contributes to their downfall. I remembered that from Blodwyn's teachings. Long ago, she had guided me through my first expulsion of a draugr. I had watched her perform the ritual flawlessly on many occasions, and when it came time for me to go out on my own, it was less than a stellar effort. "Don't worry," Blodwyn had said, "your strengths lie elsewhere. We each have our own gifts and talents. Don't let this one failure discourage you. And I wouldn't even call it a failure..."

"The boy would have died anyway," the draugr said, finishing my memory.

I pulled back a bit. "Oh. So, you're in here?" I said, pointing to my temple.

"Sometimes, yes. Sometimes, no. It comes and goes like flashes of light, like a gust of icy wind, like the paper-thin cry of the locust swelling to a crescendo then leveling off."

My face twisted in confusion for a second. "How did you know that name?"

She closed her eyes and bowed her head forward. "I know not of what you speak," she said with an agitated tone.

I placed my hand on her knee, and she quickly opened her eyes again. "Yes, you do. You said a name the first night you were here. You called out to me."

She laughed again. A low and menacing rumble from her chest. "Pink Silver," she grimaced, and her chest heaved up giving way to a wretched cough. She turned her head to the opposite side of where I knelt, spit out a gob of inky black substance, cleared her throat, and looked back at me.

"Tell me your name," I commanded.

The draugr 'tsked' her thick black tongue against the back of her teeth.

"You told Aizel! Why won't you tell me? You know my name, Trond. And you know my secret name, Ruz. It's

25

only fair if we're going to continue this relationship, don't you think?"

The draugr's voice lowered, "I told that witch nothing!" it spat. "She stole that from me. The girl was fighting hard, and there was a moment of weakness. I'm better now." It smiled again, and for a split second. There were maggots weaving in and out of its teeth. I blinked rapidly, hoping it would go away. The draugr laughed.

"So, if Aizel already knows, just tell me. What's the harm?" I pressed.

"Ask her yourself," it growled.

"I did. She won't reveal."

"And did you stop to think why?" The draugr's voice rattled my head like the quaking earth moving back and forth, shaking the trees, and startling the animals. "To her, you're still the boy. But she doesn't know. She doesn't fully realize your potential. She doesn't fully understand the power you possess."

"And what exactly is the power of my potential?"

"Hmmm," it moaned. "For the answer you seek, you must do something for me."

I raised my eyebrows inquisitively.

"Untie me. Let this body be free of these restraints before it withers and dies. That is your intent, isn't it? To let this body die? To let this girl die? To let Runa die?" That was the first time the draugr had acknowledged the name of the host it invaded.

"You know very well I can't grant that request."

"The legs then. What harm could that do? Untie these knots around this body's legs, and I will tell you what you want to know."

"Your name?"

It 'tsked' again. "That's not what you really want to know. Don't fool yourself into thinking…"

Acting on impulse, I bent back down and loosened the rope that had secured the lower body of the girl. When the last of the knots were undone, the draugr let out a deep sigh of relief with all of its many voices. It filled the room with a glorious sound that almost made me sway with the melody of it. I remained in a kneeling position directly in front of the girl and placed both my hands on top of its knees as if to lock it in place. The draugr shifted its lower body and moaned.

"Stop it!" I commanded. "I gave to you, now you give to me."

"But Ruz, your hands are so strong, I still feel…"

"Enough!" I interrupted. "Be true to your word, if you have any sense of pride."

The draugr huffed dramatically, like how a young girl would pout when not getting her way. "But don't you want to know what I want?" she whined.

"Not before you tell me what you so wisely think *I* want to know."

Her upper body relaxed, and she sighed heavily in mock defeat. "Very well then," she said meekly, and I eased up my grip on its legs a little. "But still. I don't understand. Why do you chase me and my kin from these shells? You are a heksa. A powerful one at that. Don't we share a common goal and…"

I narrowed my eyes and pressed down harder on its legs, slightly lifting myself off the backs of my feet.

"Fine," it complied. "Look to me, dear Trond. You'll see the answers in my eyes. What's important is not who I am but what I can tell you that will bring your wish to reality."

With slight hesitation, I lifted my eyes to meet hers. I knew what darkness resided there, and I had avoided direct eye contact up until that time. I had been afraid of being swept away like I was the other night. I had been afraid of being overcome with the draugr's charms. But at that moment, I knew I could no longer resist.

When our eyes locked, it was exactly as I had suspected. The draugr dug deep within my mind and held me in a vast space of time and memory. It spoke to me directly into my consciousness with its multiple, gravelly voice. But it used not the words or language of my tribe. It spoke to me with a song of the ancients—of the time before the old ones and gods had names. I was suspended in a dark void in the center of the universe and listened as the demon's voice lulled me.

"You are of the blood of a great Blodheksa," it sang, "one whose line exceeds time and space, for she was of the ancestry of the old ones. When the people first took form, her elders lay

27

with the gods, and now their blood runs through your veins. *Our* blood runs through your veins. The manner of your birth gives you dominion over the blood. You can control it. It is in you and covered you when you exited your mother's womb. Bathed in the blood. Blessed in the blood. You and your sister should have been born together, but it wasn't so. For seventeen years, you lie dormant in your mother's womb, and the balance was thrown off kilter, for there needs to be the Blood Witch and her brood to bring forth the new world. Yet, all the while, your mother knew you were there alive and well inside of her. She called you Trond—growing, stretching. You never knew your father. He was long gone before you had been born, and your mother never sought the company of another, for your father was the conduit, the bridge to help bring forth Blodwyn, the Blodsøster, and Trond, the Blodbrødre. And then you came. Bathed in blood. But the balance was skewed still, for you need the Blodheksa and her brood to bring forth the new world."

"Blodwyn?" I said out loud without realizing it.

"Ah! But you are not hers. She did not create you, and you no longer serve purpose as the Brother."

I flailed around in the vast dimension, startled, scared, confused. Fear rose to my chest. "Aizel!" I cried out. "Aizel was the Blodheksa. I, the Brother. Our union was to bring back Blodwyn, the next coming of the Sister!"

"Oh," the draugr said with finality. "Is that how you think it works?"

A blinding light bloomed in the cosmic space, and with a few blinks of my eyes, I was back in the room, kneeling before the girl.

The girl.

Runa.

The draugr's form had disappeared and before me sat the figure of the lovely girl who had arrived at the mouth of my cave three moon tides ago. I continued to blink my eyes until her full vision was no longer blurry. She was smiling at me. Gone was the cracked, gray skin. It was replaced with the smooth alabaster tones of a healthy young woman. Gone were the blackened gums and maggot-laden teeth. They were replaced with a bright and perfect white smile filled with hope and joy.

"Runa?" I inquired.

The girl rose her shoulders with an 'I don't know' gesture, and an ominous, close-mouthed smirk darkened her sweet face.

Instinctively, I blurted, "Blodwyn?"

The girl repeated her shoulder shrug and spread her legs as far apart as the arms of the chair would allow. She cocked her head back and a sultry moan escaped her throat. "Untie me. There's only one way to find out." She squirmed again, writhing her hips in my direction, offering herself to me.

Her human form was beyond compare, and the temptation stirred within me. I languidly approached her with every intention of ravaging her like the marauders in her darkest dreams. My organ was swollen and ready, and the mere thought of being intimate with this otherworldly being nearly sent me over the edge of completion.

Aizel's scolding voice stopped me in my tracks, and the girl laughed. "Trond!" Aizel admonished.

I whipped my head behind me to see Aizel standing in the threshold with six books stacked in her arms.

"A word…" she ordered.

I looked back to Runa who had closed her legs, locked her door, shut me out. She gave a small head nod in Aizel's direction. I turned on my heel and followed her out of the storage alcove.

Chapter Four

In the Time of Darkness
In the Age of Ice
Summertime, 760 AD
Caverns in the Far North
Night of the Waning Gibbous Moon

A word? To think that Aizel wanted just *a* word was ludi-crous—for it never was only singular with her. When we got to the altar at the front of the cave, she tugged on my arm, dragging me down a couple of inches so my ear was closer to her mouth. "What did you think you were doing in there with that draugr?" she hissed.

I didn't reply. It was more of a rhetorical question.

"I told you not to engage with it!"

"If *you* had, though, you would have seen what it showed me." I tried to defend myself.

"No, Trond. It would have shown me or told me what it knew *I* wanted to see and hear. The demon scans your deepest, innermost desires and…"

"It told me about my mother," I blurted. "Told me how I was born. Told me that you and I would never be able to revive Blodwyn as we had tried."

30

She shifted her weight to one leg. "You above all people know that a demon is all-knowing. Do not be fooled by its trickery."

"Just hear me out," I pleaded. "The girl, Runa. Her father said she had the sight. So, she must be special. She must be powerful. If the draugr chose her and took abode in her body, that has to mean something, right?"

Aizel sighed heavily. "No, Trond," she said with a condescending tone. "It means nothing. If a person goes into the deep too often or stays there too long, they leave themselves open for the possession to take hold. We need to let this one run its course. Let the flash fire of the draugr burn through her and eat her away until there's nothing left of her form to support it. Then it will dissipate and return to its rightful realm."

I shook my head in protest. "No. No, that isn't right. I don't believe that. I think Runa has a purpose. I cannot believe that an ancient one could last this long within her if she was just an ordinary person. We need to do the expulsion and bring her into our fold."

"You can't be serious!" she scoffed. "What power do you think the girl has?"

I pursed my lips tightly, thinking of how I was to form my next set of words, but Aizel figured it out instantly. It was written on my face.

"You think Runa is Blodwyn incarnate," she said slowly, each word dripping from her mouth like slow honey.

"It knows things," I said. "Things that only Blodwyn could know. Maybe the draugr is tapping into Runa's past life mind and waking Blodwyn up. How could it have known about the manner of my birth? Or about my father? Or about my mother?"

Aizel closed her eyes tightly, shook her head and waved her hand in the air in front of her face, as if she were trying to cancel out the noise coming from my lips. "I can't even believe you right now!" she cried, exasperated. "Of everyone, *you* should know better!" She pointed her slender forefinger at me. The tip of her pointy fingernail grazed the tip of my nose, and I jerked my head back a little to create space between us. "I thought your sister taught you better than that!"

Her words angered me, and I tried to swallow them down with a hefty gulp. "Fine," I relented, "maybe that's too extreme an assessment. But I still think the girl is valuable to us. What if she's the Blodheksa, Aizel? What if we have the Blodheksa right here, right now, under this very roof! You would rather see her rot away? Hollowed out by some demon? And besides… this draugr… what harm would it do to us? In the end, shouldn't we be working in concert with the ancient ones rather than expelling them?"

"Listen, Trond, we are not the only ones who walk the line between this world and the next. And just because there are others out there like us, doesn't mean they are *like* us. There are others who would try to subvert our power for their own gain. Don't assume that we are all on the same side. Others are jealous of our strength and seek to take it as their own. There are those who would love nothing more than to see us fail in our goal to cleanse this world. They would love nothing more than to sabotage our bloodline's mission and seek to destroy the hope of the new world we wish to create. Just because two beings walk amongst the dark doesn't mean they are kin. And as I said, you know this. You saw this happen before when Sorcia…"

I gave a little gasp in my throat without realizing it. We never talked about Sorcia. I quickly tried to change the subject. "But if Runa is…"

"She's not the Blodheksa. The Blodheksa is too powerful an entity to hold a draugr in her shell for this amount of time. The blood of the Blodheksa would have expelled it on its own by now."

There was something in her tone that made me uneasy—it was as if she didn't completely believe what she said. I raised my eyebrows, "Are you sure about that?"

"Positive." She moved closer to me and stroked my hair back away from my forehead. The small smile on her perfectly round face warmed my heart with an overwhelming sense of love and security. It brought back a rush of the old feelings I had tucked away deep in my heart for her. And her eyes were so gentle and soothing, I couldn't help but fall dreamily into them.

Since I was a little boy, Aizel had always known how to calm me down. Her magic touch was like a thousand kisses on my soul. She played the role of sister to me while my actual sister, Blodwyn, had to assume the motherly position in my life. But as I started to grow up, my feelings for Aizel began to change, and those feelings of sisterly love had turned into desire. Yet, they were not the lustful feelings I had when I mounted the armorer's daughter at the edge of the hot springs for the first time or when I entertained the naked shield master's daughters in their father's workshop. No, my exploits with other girls and women never fully amounted to the feelings I had for Aizel.

It wasn't until after Blodwyn died that Aizel and I had become passionate toward each other. I think she only surrendered to sharing my bed because she believed we were the keys to bringing Blodwyn back as the Blood Sister. But for me, it was so much more.

At that moment, as the sparks of her touch ran their course through my body, I stirred. I reached my hand up under her long red braid and pulled her close to me, hoping for a kiss, a dance between our tongues. I wanted to hold her close to me, kiss her all through the night, and feel her skin against mine. I wanted her so badly, I could hardly contain myself.

Angrily, she pulled back. "What are you doing?" she exclaimed. "Haven't you been listening to anything I've said?"

My shoulders slumped forward in defeat. She huffed again and stormed away to her section of the cave. After a few moments, I did the same.

But I was restless. I couldn't calm myself down, or settle my mind, or even put singular thoughts into a logical sequence. My brain felt jumbled, scattered. I tried to meditate, to no avail. I tried to sleep, to no avail. I tried to pleasure myself, to no avail! Finally, after what felt like an agitated eternity, I decided I would go to the place that always seemed to quell my soul—the forest.

But then Runa called to me. Her voice needled its way into my consciousness. It was low at first, too soft to be detected. And I couldn't be sure if it was her actual voice speaking out loud, or if she were directly reaching out through otherworldly channels. I crept in the darkness of the cave to spy on her in her the alcove, being sure to stay as quiet as possible. Aizel had long since been asleep. Her aura always buzzed while she was awake, and it only quieted down when slumber overtook her.

When I peeked my head into the doorway, I noticed I hadn't retied the rope around Runa's legs, and they were once again spread wide open. She smiled at me as I walked in. Her black eyes flashing in the near-pitch darkness.

"You need to be quiet," I whispered.

"I didn't say anything," she said with a giggle, directly into my mind.

I approached, knelt at her feet, and inhaled the soft scent of flowers that emitted from between her legs. Runa sighed. "Your woman doesn't want you talking to me."

"She's not my woman," I replied like an indignant child. "Not anymore."

"Never was," she chirped, but it was the draugr's voice with the multiple tones.

"Yeah, I suppose you're right."

"Still, you're not supposed to be here. But here you are, at the foot of me, thinking the most scrumptious thoughts."

I stiffened a little. "No," I defended. "I'm going to tie you back up and wait for you to wear out your welcome."

It laughed again, but the voice changed back to that of the girl. "No, you're not!" she exclaimed, and I raised a hand in front of her face to quiet her down. She gave a strained look and said, "No, you're not," this time with a hushed voice and another giggle.

I couldn't help from letting out a small laugh at the innocence of it all.

Her eyes glowed. "What do you want to know?" she asked after we had stared at each other for a few moments.

"Why her? Why this girl's body? What was so special about this one in particular?"

Runa shifted her hips in a circular motion. "Let me show you," she purred. "There is so much I can show you."

My stomach sank, and my shaft stirred, and Aizel's rejection and my inability to please myself earlier all came rushing back to me, and I gave in to my darkest temptations. Yes, I had thought about taking Runa. Yes, I had wanted to relieve myself in the most basic way I knew. Yes, I wanted to have all the carnal knowledge of this beautiful girl's body. Even though she was possessed by a draugr, *I* wanted to possess *her*.

Underneath the heavy fabric of Runa's dress, I traced the insides of her pale thighs with both my forefingers. She moaned gently as the surface of her skin bloomed with hundreds of bumps from my touch. When I reached the crevice between her legs, I pet the soft tuft of hair and smoothed it over the top of her pleasure-flesh as she wiggled a little more, trying to show my fingers where to go. But I stayed at her hair a little bit, teasing it some, until she could no longer take the featherlike brushes. I then outlined the ridges to the opening of her sex. She was slick with desire as I softly stroked her area up and down with two fingers. Her honey coated my fingertips and she continued to moan and writhe at my touch. I leaned in, wrapped my left arm around the chair, turned my right hand at her sex palm up, and inserted my middle and forefinger inside of her. I rested my face in the crook of her lap as I pumped her slowly with butterfly thrusts, changing my rhythm to match how she moaned and bucked against me. Fast, then slow, gentle, then hard. My fingers massaged the soft pad at the top of her insides, and soon her pleasure burst all over my fingers. She threw her head back and squealed, and at the same time, I saw flashes of images in my mind's eye. Fires, and explosions, and dead bodies dancing from tree limbs. One by one, the onslaught of visions heightened my senses and hardened my manhood into a frenzy.

"I can show you so much more," she whispered. "I know you want to see."

I released my hold on her, stood up, and untied the shackles at her upper torso. "Not here," I whispered and lifted her from the chair.

She was like a feather to pick up—weightless—and I held her like a baby in my arms and brought her out into the forest, all the while wondering how the draugr had not yet consumed this waif of a girl already. The night air was cool, but neither of us were disturbed by it, for our heat ignited the second I swooped her up and we exited the cave. Deep in the woods, I brought her to my special place—the spot where I always had felt safe and protected.

I laid her down on the ground, and my urge to take her was so strong that I found myself in a red frenzy tearing at the buttons of her dress, frantically trying to rip it off her. My need, my desire to touch her skin and feel it radiate off and into me was uncontrollable. She merely laughed at my fumbling motions. "Easy, Ruz."

I pulled back. "Don't call me that. My sister called me that. You're not her."

"Easy, Trond," she corrected, and her voice hypnotized me. It washed over me like a warm stream of water cleansing away all my sins.

I laid on top of her and furiously kissed her, darting my tongue deep into her mouth. She accepted my kisses and gave me her tongue in return. I nipped her lips with my teeth, and she answered in kind in a reckless and frenetic dance. She tasted like berries from the bush, succulent and sweet, and I ran my tongue over the roof of her mouth to try to savor that flavor. Runa spread her legs around me and ran her hands down my back. When she got to my backside, she pushed me into her, and my organ, sheathed with the fabric of my pants, tried angrily to find its way to her opening. I bucked my hips wildly, trying to free it from its cage, and she laughed at me again. "No wonder she still thinks you a boy."

I bit down hard on her lip, drawing a sliver of blood. "Boy?" I howled in her crook of her neck. "Boy?"

She reached one arm up and underneath me and tilted my chin, so I looked her directly in the eyes. The blackness there churned, sparkled, twisted, and changed. I blinked a few times to snap my vision into focus. "Oh no," she gushed. "So much more. Not boy, nor man, but beast on stormy shores." Her voice lulled me again, and she curled her legs to the waistband of my pants, used her toes to latch onto the fabric, and shimmied them down my thighs. My organ was at attention and within reach of her.

"Show me everything. I want to see," I said.

And as I plunged myself into her, she brushed her palm over my forehead and ran her fingers through my hair, which sent the visions to my mind. She showed me everything as my body rocked with each pleasurable wave.

Runa clawed at my back as I drove myself deep into her crevice. Her warmth and wetness consumed me from tip to base, and with each plunge, with each time I pulled out of her only to drive deeper still, the sticky secretions of hers emptied out and coated every inch of me to the insides of my thighs. She had a heat like no other—like fire blazing between her legs, and I grinded myself deep, deeper, deepest, to cleanse myself in it. There was an unnatural feeling to how slick she was, but I ignored the oddness of it and enjoyed how I was able to slide in and out with ease.

"Take her," she said in the draugr's voice—deep and guttural like it was growling across space and time. I ignored the strangeness of that too and planted my hands into the ground to position myself for better leverage. The pleasure was rising quickly and intensely, as I had never experienced before. "Take her like the beast you are," it said again, "for she has never been ridden like this." Runa's sex clamped hard against me, nearly locking me in place like a tight vice. But I didn't let that stop my feverish thrusts. She arched her hips, inviting me to go even deeper. I didn't think was possible, but it was. To my amazement, it was! I rode her harder, and faster, and more desperately, like I was going to split her wide open and create an opening in the sky. In my mind's eye, the stars collided with bright flashes of light, and in its wake a glowing gash tore apart a wide opening, much like the one between Runa's legs. And from it spewed devils, demons, and rainbows made of fire, and fountains of blood—a steady onslaught of devastation and destruction outpouring and overflowing from the beyond world into ours. It was so beautiful. Every time I pounded into Runa's sex, a new image sprang from the starry opening in the sky.

Runa arched her back and screamed out in ecstasy. "The stars have moved!" she exclaimed in her human voice. I opened my eyes and looked at her. Her mouth was agape with sheer wonder and awe as if she had just awoken to the most fantastical sight before her. Her eyes were wide and sparkling with the reflection of the cluster of stars formed in the sky. She saw it too, exactly what I saw in my head. She reached her arm out as if to touch the stars. "They're mine!" she moaned with delight. "Give them to me, Trond! Help me reach the stars."

At that, I slowed my pace and worked in and out of her opening gently and steadily to bring myself to the full apex of my pleasure. I withdrew with a lingering, deliberate motion, savoring her heat and the saturation of her secretions all over me, and then I slid slowly back in, making her feel every ridge of my powerful cock deep inside her. Her sex swallowed me, and I eased in and out of her, each time making her moan louder and flail herself in time with my plunges. Then, her body tensed, and her insides swelled up around me. One last time, her sex fastened onto my shaft, and she exploded with delight. I remained inside, giving one last internal jab before I emptied myself into her cavity. I cried out from the intense eruption as my body quivered, relaxed, and fell on top of her. She kissed my ear lightly and bid me to slide out.

Bathed in blood, I heard a voice say. It wasn't the voice of the draugr, or Runa, or even me. It was different, one I hadn't heard before. One that seemed to come from the trees, or the gash in the sky that was quickly disappearing.

I wiggled from Runa and sat up and, in the darkness, noticed I was not just covered in Runa's moisture, but I was covered in blood—deep red and thick. It coated me from the waist down to where my pants had been pulled halfway to my knees. I looked to Runa, and she was bathed in it, too— the insides of her thighs, and the little box of slick black hair between her legs.

Covered. Coated. Bathed.

Runa sat up with her legs still bent at the knees and examined the scene at her crevice. She lowered her hand, plunged her fingers insides herself with a little moan, then pulled them out and brought them to her lips. They were bloody fingers attached to gray, cracked hands, and I knew she had transformed again. With a thick black tongue, the draugr licked the fingers clean, then laughed—its voice piercing through the trees in the forest and carried along the night air.

My stomach did a violent lurch, and I turned my head to the side so I could throw up.

Chapter Five

In the Time of Darkness
In the Age of Ice
Summertime, 760 AD
Caverns in the Far North
Night of the Half Moon

Four moon tides passed, and with each one, I went to her—my dark, mistress lover in the woods. And after each one of our clandestine escapades, I returned her to her spot in the alcove of our cave and retied her shackles as if nothing had gone molested. For four indulgent nights, the draugr catered to every one of my deepest desires and left no terrain off-limits. Anything I wanted to do to it and *with* it was fair game. She encouraged my twisted suggestions and let me put myself wherever I pleased. She took part in my indecent cravings and let me use her body for my every whim. Our blood and bodily fluids were surely a site to behold blanketing the forest grounds. I had never felt the extreme pain and pleasure like that from Runa's sheer will. She drove me continuously to the edge of ecstasy like waves on distant shores and brought me visions of the old ones and the new world I had sought to create every time we tore open the starry hole in the sky with our ungodly fornication.

Chapter Five

Soon, though, I found myself daydreaming about our nightly jaunts and had become distracted. I obsessed over the thought of plunging myself into her every orifice. I found myself craving every inch of her—her scent, her touch, her tight sex clamped around my cock. But my thoughts started to turn more sinister as I visualized not only consuming her in a carnal, metaphorical way, but also in an actual *consuming* way—teeth scraping and tearing at her flesh, eating her sex and *eating* her sex. At first, the thoughts bothered me, but the more they took root in my mind, the more *Runa* took root in my mind, the more natural they felt. Something inside me told me these feelings weren't right—that the desires I yearned for weren't solely of my volition. I briefly thought, am I being possessed? But that thought only made my well-spent cock stiff again with delight. I laughed it off.

On the fifth moon tide, I stumbled back to the cave naked with Runa in my arms. I draped her dress over her head and tied her back to the chair like I had done so many times. She was spent, limp, unresponsive. I wrapped the ropes around her frail body and doubled the knots for good measure. No. I just wanted to inflict a little bit more pain. This night had been particularly violent, and while the draugr's passion and heat were equally matched with mine, the deteriorating body of the human girl had been quickly faltering. It was apparent the demon's hold on her would soon be her demise. But I didn't care. I didn't care that the draugr showed me its true monster face when we laid together or that she covered me in maggots when she rode me. I didn't care. I didn't care. I didn't care. And if that meant I was a slave to the demon, I didn't care about that either.

I pushed Runa's shoulder back one more time to see if she would wake, but she was out cold. There was still a fire inside me though, and even though she had satisfied me tenfold, I was still hungry with passion. I wanted more, and I was poised and ready to penetrate anyone or anything had they presented themselves to me. I stood before the comatose girl and stroked myself, hoping the self-pleasure would ease my flames, but it was no use—I was too worked up.

41

And then I thought of Aizel sound asleep in her space, and it had been so long since we'd been together. I thought about her soothing touches and gentle kisses and how she always made me feel warm, loved, and special. The soft red hair between her legs was always inviting and thinking about her sex hungrily and happily accepting my shaft was all I needed to visit her bed.

I crept quietly, loomed in her archway for a moment or two, then tiptoed my way in so I wouldn't wake her. Gently, I pulled back her bearskin blanket and marveled at her flawless, naked body. The rush of the summer breeze filtered in through the cave, but she didn't even flinch from the air licking her exposed flesh. She was on her stomach with her arms folded underneath her breasts so that the weight of her bosom and torso was balanced under her sleeping spot, and the curve of her back gave way to the voluptuous mound of her backside, like a milky white hill begging to be explored. She was perfect and pure—not like my demon lover covered in blood and filth. Aizel was a goddess. An old one of pure light.

I swept her long red hair to the side, crawled on top of her, and slowly kissed her shoulder blades. She gave a small moan and shifted slightly beneath me as I ran my mouth to the small of her back. I grazed my tongue just at the top of the line where the dimples of her lower half connect to the vertical crease of her backside, when suddenly she shot up from her slumber and whipped her upper body.

A look of fury overcame her face, and her eyes turned red with rage. "Trond!" she screamed. "Get off me right now!"

Her voice shook me to my core, and my body jolted as I jumped up from her sleeping spot. My head was fuzzy, and I felt sick in my stomach like I had been drinking a strong brew all day. I didn't know where I was or what I was doing, and the room spun around with a violent turn. From the alcove, I heard the draugr laughing—its voice like a song from the depths of the underworld.

Aizel leaned down, picked up up her bearskin blanket, and wrapped it around herself.

"I... I... I didn't know wha..." I started to say.

"Didn't know what you were doing? Are you about to tell me you didn't know what you were doing?"

I had no response. I sat on the floor with my back against the wall and curled my knees to my chest like a child being punished.

"Trond! Look at me!" she said forcefully, and I raised my eyes to meet hers. She bent forward, took my chin in her hands, and came close to my face, practically nose to nose. "Come out of there!" she commanded me.

In my haziness, I barely understood what she meant, and I glared at her.

"The gray of your eyes is too dark," she mumbled and knelt closer. Her blanket fell from her shoulders, yet her nakedness didn't seem to be a priority at that moment for she didn't try to pull it on.

I tried to respond, truly I did, but I was paralyzed, and Runa was laughing so loudly it all but drowned out Aizel's voice.

"Trond!" she yelled again. "Trond!" She shook my shoulders.

I opened my mouth to say, "Stop yelling in my face, Aizel," but that proved fruitless. My lips moved, but no sound came from them.

"That's good," she said. "That's very good." And again, I didn't understand. "Listen to my voice, Trond. I'm coming for you."

She placed both her hands on each side of my head and covered my ears. The world seemed to stop, and my heart seemed to stop, and Aizel's visage slowly went out of focus until I could see nothing but black.

In that blackness, Aizel's footprints scampered around my head frantically searching for me. But like a little boy playing a joke, I was hiding in the darkest part of the forest. Every time she passed a clearing in the woods, she was able to see the visions and me and my demon lover during our various tableaus of unnatural intercourse. Everything I had kept secret from Aizel was now there in plain sight as she traipsed around my consciousness, but she paid those scenes no mind, for she had one mission and that was to find me in the woods. "Trond!" she cried out. "Trond, I know you're here."

43

My heart felt a sudden rush of shame, and I tucked myself behind a silver tree. I didn't want her to see me. I couldn't face her. Not after she had seen what I had done.

"It's alright, Trond," her voice echoed. "Come out, and I will keep you safe. We will both make this right. It's not your fault. Let me help you."

I looked up to the sky and saw the half-moon shining down on me. Its half face was jagged and ridged and its mouth opened wide with laughter. The draugr's laughter. I tried to cover my ears to shut the sound out, but no matter what I did, I couldn't escape it. The clouds suddenly covered the view of the moon, and the forest went dark and cold. A thick layer of ice churned up from the forest floor, locking my feet in place. I panicked. My breaths came in labored pants, and I was sure I was going to pass out.

"Don't go there, Trond," Aizel said with a reassuring tone. "Don't listen to it. Don't fall prey to it. You are stronger than that. You are stronger than all of it. Remember, keep your good thoughts flowing, right? Isn't that what Blodwyn always said? Blodwyn, Trond—the Blood Sister. *Your* sister. We still have work to do, you and I. Now come on out, and let's finish what we started!"

The thick ice crept up to my ankles and made its way to my knees, and I surely thought once it reached my chest it would freeze my heart forever. But the conviction in Aizel's words, the mention of Blodwyn's legacy, and my own sheer will and determination brought my mind back into focus.

My sister was the greatest witch I had ever known.

"Yes," Aizel replied.

My sister was the best Blodsøster to step foot in this human realm.

"Yes," Aizel responded.

And my sister will come again—she will be born into this world and lead us to paradise.

"Amen," Aizel said, but it wasn't Aizel's voice nor the draugr's. It was musical and melodious—a great surge of voices ringing out as one. It was a voice of a hundred heksas bowing down at Blodwyn's feet, praising her name. I knew the word— amen— but it was foreign to me, and I had no use for it, but it felt... *right*. It felt appropriate, like a closing of a ritual, or an affirmation of our faith and dedication to the old ones.

Before I had a chance to respond in kind, I opened my eyes wide. I was no longer in the forest hiding behind a tree, no longer slowly being encased in a thick layer of ice. Aizel was in front of me, stroking my hair. Her eyes were calming and filled with relief and joy. "Oh, there you are," she said brightly. "I knew you'd come home."

"I'm so..." I started to croak, but she cut me off.

"Hush. Say no more."

"But I almost..."

"I said to hush!" she insisted. "Trust me, do you think you could have even if you tried?" she said with a sly smirk.

I smiled back and lowered my head. "No," I relented. "But I still am so sorry that I even attempted..."

"It wasn't really you, though. We both know that. Can we just agree that when it comes to draugrs, you'll listen to me from now on?"

I let out half a chuckle followed with a sigh. "You saw, didn't you?"

Aizel nodded. "Aye."

"Everything?"

She raised her eyebrows in concern. "Yes, Trond. I saw everything."

"That's what I thought," I muttered with a hint of shame. "So now what? Where do we go from here?"

"In terms of us, or in terms of the draugr?"

I stiffened a little. "Oh, I was thinking in terms of the draugr, but..."

She plopped her bottom on the ground and crisscrossed her legs in front of her. "I think it's appropriate to start there," she said, cutting me off. "At this point we'll probably have to attempt an expulsion,

"Expulsion? But you said to let the demon run its course. Let the draugr consume the girl and go back to whence it came. Why would that change now?"

"You changed it, Trond. The intimate physical contact you had with it changed everything. If we let the draugr burn out and release back into the cosmos, I'm afraid that won't be the last we see or hear of it. It stained you. You're attached to it now, and I worry that for the rest of your life it will try to take hold of your power. Because that's all it really wants from you, you know. Your power as an Aevir causes it to lust for you."

I shake my head. "Yes, but then how would an expulsion be any different?"

"When the demon is exorcised, *we* leave our mark on *it*. For them, it's like a mark of shame. We put our stain on them. Other draugrs don't take kindly to that."

"So, wouldn't an exorcised demon just return to me regardless? Do you understand what I'm saying, Aizel? Either way, it still very well may continue its attack on us."

Aizel placed her elbows on the tops of her knees and rested her chin in the palms of her hands on either side of her cheeks. "I know. These are the things I've been working through in my head. There may be a solution, but I still need to run the test on the girl before I do anything."

"What test?" I crowed.

"Um…" she stammered, "how many nights did you lay with her? And it was multiple times per night, correct?"

I lowered my head.

"If she is with child," she paused, inhaled, then released her breath noisily, "*your* child…" her voice trailed off, and I opened my mouth to protest, but she cut me off again. "Was that the plan? Some crazy scheme to bring forth Blodwyn? Did you think your blood, the blood of the Blodbrødre, mixed with the draugr and your heksa power, could bring Blodwyn into life?"

Yes, I wanted to say, but the shame was too consuming. Aizel was right. And when she laid it out in such a way, it sounded like an idiotic plan. "I don't know," I managed. "I don't know what I was thinking."

Aizel stood up. "Well, it definitely had you under its thrall, there's no mistaking that."

I rose as well.

"Go back to your quarters and get dressed. Then meet me in the alcove with the girl. I'll need your help with the test."

I did as Aizel asked and within minutes, we reconvened in the storage room where Runa was kept. Her eyes blinked open when I entered, and she smiled as I stood before her. The draugr had mustered up enough energy to present in its human form, and my heart almost fluttered at the lovely site of my pleasure waif.

Aizel arrived shortly after clad in her cloth dress and carrying items from the altar. "Hold this for me," she said as she handed me a wooden bowl. In it was a thin wooden stick with a point at the end, and an egg-shaped stone the size of a fist that had beautiful gold and blue hues: Labradorite, a sacred gem for the northern heksas.

Aizel walked behind Runa.

"Oh," Runa said, but she spoke with the voice of the draugr. "I see we've decided to try to get rid of me, is that so?"

Aizel eyed me sharply—a warning not to answer the demon.

"Sweet Ruz," the draugr cooed. "No love for me now?"

"Shut up!" I snapped.

"Trond!" Aizel scolded and plucked a strand of hair from Runa's head at the root then walked back to me.

"Ow!" the demon feigned pain, then laughed.

Aizel reached into the bowl, pulled out the stick, and wound the strand of long black hair around it tight enough so it stayed in place.

Aizel turned back to me. "Kiss me," she commanded.

Taken off guard, I tried to respond but couldn't. Runa stirred in her chair. A little gasp escaped her mouth. Was that a gasp of jealousy?

"I said kiss me, Trond," Aizel repeated. "Kiss me now."

Without further hesitation, I leaned into her and planted my mouth upon hers. Her tongue welcomed mine heartily, and we were in perfect time and rhythm. My cock hardened quickly against my trousers, and Aizel ran her hand across the outline of my bulge.

Runa bounced in her chair like a petulant child. "What is this?" she demanded. "Are you trying to make me jealous? Or are you getting ready for me to join you?" But we ignored the demon and continued to be swept away in our enthusiastic kiss.

"Touch me," Aizel moaned, and grabbed my free hand and guided it to her breast. On the outside of her dress, I squeezed one, then the other. I took each nipple between my fingers and pinched them. She squealed in delight, and my shaft raged and pulsed, begging me to let it out.

"Not nice," the draugr pouted. "I'm feeling left out." Again, we ignored its pleas.

"Touch me," Aizel moaned again, and with her free hand she lifted her dress to expose her naked body to me. Swiftly, my hand dipped between her legs. The heat and moisture from her sex were like diving into a hot spring, and I wasted no time pushing two fingers deep inside her. She kissed me harder as I moved in and out of her, and as the pleasure overtook her core she could barely stand upright. With my thumb, I gently massaged the soft knob on the outside of her sex simultaneously in rhythm with my fingers pumping her, but before she could come to completion, she wriggled her hips away, bidding me to slide out.

"Wait! Wait!" the draugr cried. "She's not done yet!" And again, we ignored it.

Aizel reached into the bowl, removed the egg-shaped crystal, and handed it to me. Its blue and gold colors glowed and shimmered in the torchlight of the room, mesmerizing me with its shape, girth, and colorful splendor. I knew immediately what Aizel intended for me to do, so I granted her wish, held the stone tightly at the bottom end, and used the tip of the gem to rim the outline of her opening. Her chest fluttered with the cold touch of the stone to her flesh. Tenderly, methodically, I inserted the curved part into her. She flinched at the initial entry of the object, but I eased it into her gently. Slowly at first, she moved in time with my pressure on it. In and out, in and out, I pumped the stone inside gradually going higher and higher into her. I worked the large gem as if I were thrusting her with my own organ—lovingly but forcefully enough to grind against all her soft pleasure spots. She moaned and squealed and panted in spite of herself, and she cried out "Yes! Yes!" with reckless abandon just as the stone was fully inserted inside. My palm sealed over her opening, pressing the full force of the crystal inside and locking it in place within her. Her hips rocked, and her legs quivered, and her breathing was like quickened spasms.

A minute or so later, she relaxed her stance, and the gem fell into my hand covered with her juices. She took it from me and placed it back in the bowl.

The draugr was silent, wild-eyed, with a darkened expression on its face. "Oh, you heksas," it growled. "You and your rituals. You and your traditions. You have no idea what it's like. You have no idea what it was to rule this land, and…" Its words ended on a high-note squeal as Aizel had used the pointed end of the stick wrapped with Runa's hair to draw blood from the girl's bound finger.

"Hush your mouth, and relax," Aizel ordered, and she squeezed three drops of the girl's blood onto the labradorite in the bowl.

I watched as Aizel dangled the rod above it. The stick spun around and around, and she examined the contents within. Finally, when the stick stopped, Aizel looked up at me with a smile, and I sighed with relief.

I had not impregnated the demon.

But the question now remained: do we let the draugr run its course, or attempt an expulsion after all?

Chapter Six

In the Time of Darkness
In the Age of Ice
Summertime, 760 AD
Caverns in the Far North
Night of the Waning Crescent Moon

After the realization—and celebration—that Runa was not with child had set in and filled us with much happiness, the next task of how to deal with the draugr took over. The two options we had—expelling the demon, or letting it consume the girl to nothing—didn't seem like they would be fruitful in the long term. The possibility that the demon would always be a part of our lives was very real, and Aizel and I had no concrete answers on how to manage that.

A few days after she had given the test to Runa, Aizel awoke with a new sense of purpose. She told me that the answer had come to her in a dream, but she would need a few days to prepare everything for the ceremony. In the meantime, I was to travel into the village and bring the girl's father, Sten, back to the cave. He would not be a participant in the exorcism, but as soon as the ritual was complete, it would be necessary for him to immediately take her away from us. She didn't explain any of the particular details but only said the voice in her dream spoke to her as if from far away—as if through

time and space. Her words chilled me, for I had heard a voice like that before, one that broke the barrier of the cosmos and pierced my consciousness like a sharp-bladed sword.

I was worried to leave her, even if it would only be for a few days. I worried for her safety—being alone with the draugr and all. She tsked her tongue at me and waved her hand dismissively in the air. "You think I've never been alone with a draugr before?"

I threw my hands up and shrugged. "I had, too. It was nothing new for me but look what happened. I think it is safe to say this is a whole different beast we're dealing with."

"I'll be fine," she reassured. "Besides, I have so much to do, the draugr won't even be a distraction. Now go. Get her fodir here. We can't do the ceremony without him nearby. The voice was truly clear about that."

I nodded and left at once.

On my way to the village, I realized that it had been some time since I had left the surrounding area of my cave. Maybe because I had been too consumed with resurrecting my sister Blodwyn. Maybe because I had just become so weary with ordinary people and relished in my own little world of power and magic. Maybe I felt I was better than everyone else—as an Aevir, I would live many, many lives, while the people around me withered and died. Maybe it was a combination of all three. Yet, as I traversed the huts and tents, and makeshift campsites of our village, I began to take notice of how things had changed—transformed. There was a different energy in the air, like something had shifted. Scanning the faces of the groups of people huddled together, I could barely recognize who anyone was. Age had taken its hold on many of them, time had torn many up or laid them on the pyre. New and unfamiliar life sprang in their place. And they stared at me— like an outsider, like an outcast. Some of the elders gasped when I passed them by, and Aizel's words came crashing back to me: *"The people in the villages are starting to talk. They've always talked, but this time it's louder."*

As quickly as I could, I contacted Sten. He had been camping alongside the armorer's station and wasn't hard to spot. His black hair indicated he was different – an outsider.

51

The armorer asked if I wanted to rest and spend the night, but his uneasy mannerism around me made me decline his offer. The day's trek home wouldn't be so arduous with a companion, I had explained, and besides, we needed to be on our way because Aizel had plans to work us to the bone. "Women!" the armorer had huffed, and we all gave a small uncomfortable chuckle. As we walked back through the village and headed for home, I didn't feel as much an outsider with him by my side.

Sten wasn't much for conversation during our journey back, which I didn't mind at all. He asked how Runa was doing and what the progress was like concerning the ritual. I told him she was fine, we were nearing the end of things, and it would all be over soon—which was a half-truth. Runa was not fine, nor would she ever be again, I surmised.

When we reached the cave, I instructed him to stay outside. "No matter what you hear, no matter the screams, or cries, or false statements that pour from the draugr's mouth, you must always remain out here. You cannot go in. Your presence can potentially destroy any progress we make with expelling the demon."

Sten's black eyes widened with fear. "I understand," he muttered. "Just bring my girl back to me, please."

Upon entering the cave, it was obvious Aizel was ready to begin the exorcism. The altar was illuminated with the free-standing torches at its sides. A brazier in the center burned brightly and the scent of one of Aizel's herbal concoctions wafted in the air. In the center of the open room, Runa, the draugr, sat tied to her chair inside a circle of salt and rocks with painted runes. I had barely stepped all the way inside when Aizel whipped her body around and smiled anxiously at me. "Oh great! You're finally here! Is the fodir with you?"

"Yes. I instructed him to stay out there no matter what."

She nodded tersely with focus and determination. "What's the moon status right now?"

"Crescent. Few clouds."

"Stars?" she asked as she ground a white marble pestle deep into a black granite mortar.

"Clear," I answered.

"You know all about the stars, don't you, Ruz?" the draugr's voice chuckled.

Aizel's eyes opened wide. "Oh!" she exclaimed in mock surprise. "Someone decided to join the ceremony!"

I cocked my head to the side in confusion.

"Oh, it's nothing," Aizel dismissed. "Someone here wasn't being cooperative, so I had to conjure up one of my teas so she would be more … compliant."

Runa violently thrashed her shoulders against the rope. "Stupid witch!" she spat.

"Never you mind," Aizel sang as she continued with her work.

I walked up to the altar passing the outer rim of the sacred circle and Runa eyed me seductively. One-half of her face was riddled with opened, oozing blisters. The other half was gray and cracked with the eyeball almost completely sunken deep into the socket. She was skeletal, and I wondered how, or if, the actual girl was still alive.

"She's still here," the draugr cooed, reading my thoughts. "You know you want a taste." She flicked her black tongue in and out rapidly like a snake.

I crinkled my nose at the offensive scent coming from the circle. "She stinks," I complained to Aizel.

"Yeah, well, they all stink in the end, don't they," Aizel replied with an airy sigh.

I shrugged slightly in agreement. "So, what's the plan? If I were to guess it, this has all the dressings of a normal expulsion. I thought this was supposed to be different. What about your dream and the grand novel approach?"

Aizel put the mortar and pestle down at the altar and reached for an object next to the brazier. A metal object attached to a black leather strap lay in a piece of fabric, and as the scent of iron made its way to my nostrils, I immediately knew the cloth had been previously saturated in blood. I narrowed my eyes in doubt and suspicion. "This," she declared proudly.

"What is it?" I asked.

"Stupid witch! Stupid, weak witch!" Runa yelled from the circle.

Aizel rolled her eyes in disgust at the draugr's outburst, then turned her attention back to me and smiled with pride. "Hold out your hand," she beamed as she shook the piece of silver from the blood-stained rag and into my palm.

Instantly, a pulse of energy rushed up my arm and up to one side of my neck. A ringing sound sharply filled my ear with a high-pitched tone, then tapered off to a low-humming din. My hand felt heavy, weighted down, with the object in it. But *I* felt weightless at the same time. Whatever magics Aizel had conjured and constructed, I had no words for. I was in awe of her ability to wield it so.

"That is a container," she said. "Fashioned with steel, blessed with our spells, dedicated to the old ones."

Runa's maniacal laughter filled the cave like a thousand voices rising from the depths of the underworld. I winced slightly to try to block the sound from my ears. "Stupid witch thinks she can hold me? Stupid cow thinks she can trap me in a necklace?"

I held the object by its leather cord and dangled it in front of my eyes to inspect it. It swung side to side, and I was mesmerized by it, hypnotized by the shimmering metal glinting the light from the torches in the cave. "An eye," I said. "It looks like an eye."

Aizel swiftly reached for the object with the blood rag and wrapped it up again. "It's not an eye," she huffed defensively.

"Then what on earth is it?"

"It's a burrowing insect. One that emerges once every generation to cause destruction and death."

"The paper-thin cry of the locust," the draugr sang.

"Hush!" I screamed at Runa. "I don't know, Aizel. Looks like an eye to me."

Her face flushed hot with anger and embarrassment. "Oh, whatever!" she cried, and held onto the necklace. "I made it for you. You were in my head when I melted and shaped the steel. It was the first thing I thought of."

I placed a hand on her shoulder and smiled. "Thank you," I said gently. "It's very sweet. But is it safe?"

Her eyes flashed green to blue. "Do you mean, will it hold the draugr?"

Runa raged against the ropes. "Nothing! Nothing! Nothing can hold me!" It screamed louder this time—so loud that Aizel shut her eyes and covered her ears.

"I think we should start," I finally said after Runa settled down.

"I agree," Aizel responded, and we both took our marks outside the circle.

Aizel unwrapped the necklace and placed the bloody cloth at her feet. "Runa," she began. "Draugr. I cast you out of this mortal coil." She raised her hand with the necklace in it and dangled the charm in the air.

"New magic," the draugr spat. "New magic won't work, stupid witch."

"In this circle, I invoke the old ones. In this circle, I invoke the ancients who came before us and who will come again. Help me cleanse the girl called Runa and return her to her former self. Send this filthy draugr back to the depths of its suffering and pain."

"I'm the filthy one?" Runa said calmly. "Me? Yet, you're the ones who want to open the gates and let the chaos flood into this world. Let's not try to fool ourselves here—we are only acting for our own desires and pleasures." She leaned her head backward to where I stood and looked at me with her upside-down face. "Isn't that right, Ruz?" Her voice was like knives against my ears, scraping away all the soft spots on the inside of me.

I remained eyes forward, connected with Aizel as she spoke the spells with the old words of our brethren. The ancient tongue had been gifted to her long ago, and while I knew not the words she spoke and knew not the definitions and translations, I knew what they meant—I felt them in the deepest pit of my soul, and I understood them at the most basic level in my subconscious.

Suddenly, a sharp pain struck me at the base of my skull and worked its way up to the top of my head. It was a creeping pain, like sharp nails dragging across granite. My vision shifted, and I saw the outside forest with the trees dancing low to the ground, covering up the view of stars in the sky. The moon's sliver of a smile only showed itself partially, and

I strained my eyes to see it in its full glory. But I could not, for the draugr was manipulating my thoughts, whittling its way into the deepest recesses of my mind. I tried to ignore it, to push it away, to fight against the needling sensations, but it was strong, and without my full concentration, I was powerless against it.

Aizel saw me struggle. The look on my face must have given away that something was amiss, and she recited a line with unfaltering conviction.

Sensing our weakened defenses, the draugr laughed, "You know what he did to me out there in the woods," it crowed. "He wants to do it again."

Aizel ignored it and continued on.

The draugr breathed heavily and with a mighty jolt of its lower body, the chair bounced off the stone floor and the ropes at its lap broke free. Runa laughed and spread her legs open. The smell of rot and decay caught me at the back of my throat, and I stepped back an inch to free myself from the stench, Aizel remained unfazed.

The draugr rotated its hips suggestively. "He licked me there," it purred. "A pity because I don't think he ever did that to you, did he? And it felt so good. Made all my maggots squirm at once. Hmmm... as a matter of fact, he wanted to eat me. Gnash his teeth against my flesh and devour this body. He almost did, Aizel. He still wants to, don't you Ruz? Chew it slow. Savor it. Lick your lips, little worm. Like how we did to the modir. We ate her." Its voice went deep and rumbly. "We ate her. Ingested her screams. Devoured her soul. She's here with us now, too, you know. She's still screaming."

The draugr tilted its head back and opened its mouth. From it came a hideous and frightened scream of a woman— Runa's mother. Gyda. Again, I winced at the sound, but Aizel remained steadfast in her place.

"Shut up," I whispered under my breath, but the draugr winked at me with its good eye and propped its head up to face Aizel.

"Your spells won't work, heksa," it taunted. "You know who I am. You know I can't be contained. You're nothing but a poor excuse for a witch. Your power is nothing! Your power means nothing. You are nothing! You're not even good enough to bear fruit. You're not even worthy to be the Blodheksa!"

"Shut up!" I said louder.

"Trond!" Aizel admonished and continued the spell, but I knew the draugr's words were starting to get to her.

"Say my name, filthy heksa," the draugr continued. "Oh, that's right you don't want..."

Quickly, I looked at Aizel and my face twisted with suspicion. "What are you keeping from me?" my eyes pleaded.

It was Aizel's turn to scream, "Shut up!" And a strong wind blew through the cave and extinguished the torches.

A voice called "Runa!" from the opening. It was poor, scared Sten, in fear for the safety of his child.

"You can't save her, you have to know that much, at least," the draugr growled.

A fire took over within Aizel's eyes, and instantly, the torches were relit.

The draugr hummed a little. "Nice trick. When you meet your end, heksa, let it be known that it will be the same fire to send you into oblivion."

"Maybe so, draugr," Aizel snarled through gritted teeth. "But that day is but lifetimes away, for I was gifted the power of the Aevir—a power you so wish to possess." She gingerly raised her foot in the air and began to cross over into the circle.

"Wait! Aizel! Don't!" I yelled in protest.

"Never mind that, Trond. You need to leave now," she commanded, her eyes trained on the hideous face of the broken girl. The necklace with the silver pendant was clutched tightly in her hand.

"You can't..." I said in protest.

"Leave! I'm not going to tell you again. Get out of here! Now!" Her voice rang out in the cave, and with fear in my heart, I raced out. I looked back only once, and the last thing I saw was Aizel fully stepping into the circle with the demon. And the screams and growls, chants, and unnatural voices that blared out into the night sky would forever stay fresh in my mind.

Aizel dangled the necklace in the space between us. It hummed a low hum of reverberation in my head with every movement it made. Forward and back, the din was deep and unnoticeable to the average ear. I could not only hear its noise, but I felt it. It was like a heavy rumble deep inside the earth, slightly shaking the guts of the ground.

Runa lay sprawled on the floor. She breathed still, but it was faint and barely noticeable. When Sten had been permitted to come back into the cave, he was convinced she was dead. Aizel had to take a flat piece of stone up to her nose to show him a thin line of moisture as residue of her breathing. Runa lived. Hardly. Aizel knelt beside Runa and looped the cord with the pendant around her neck. "She is to keep this on," Aizel instructed Sten. "It is hers now. She holds the draugr. It is a sign for anything from the beyond to keep away from her."

Sten wept and picked up Runa's motionless body and cradled her in his arms like a baby. "Thank you! Thank you!" he exclaimed with praise. "I don't know how I can repay you. I have nothing to give."

"Your gratitude is enough," Aizel said humbly.

"I will sing your praises to everyone I meet!" he said as the tears of joy streamed down his face. "Your names will be known throughout the land!"

Aizel gave a tight-lipped smile, but her eyes went dark. "You are too kind."

"Thank you, again," Sten said. He bowed to both of us, pulled Runa closer to his chest and left.

"Will it work?" I asked when the man was out of earshot. "Can the demon escape it?"

"It'll work," Aizel replied matter-of-factly. "The draugr won't escape unless someone like us wills it so."

"Another Aevir?"

Aizel nodded. "Only an Aevir like us can wield that power. Control it. Make the draugr do our bidding. And we would have the power to unleash it, although I don't know why we would."

"But its power. The necklace is seething with it."

"Oh, I have no doubt it will be a curse on that girl's family. The power within it can only be tempered by those like us. I'm sure many will succumb to that darkness."

"Controlled by other heksas," I mused.

"There are all types of heksas, Trond. The world over breeds them. All different kinds of heksas with different abilities not of this world. But we have enemies. There are those who are in direct opposition of our cause and those who would strive for our power as Aevir." Her voice trailed off with a faraway tone. It made me uncomfortable to hear that timbre.

"You make it sound like we're at war," I said with a chuckle, trying to lighten the mood.

She placed her hands on my shoulders and looked directly into my eyes. "But we are, Trond. It's us against them. You heard what Sten said. He is going to talk about us to anyone and everyone who'll listen. He'll call us by our names and tell the people what we did... what we *can* do. There will be some who won't believe him, some who will be grateful for our existence, and some who will want to hunt us down and snuff us out. The world is changing, Trond."

I remembered the other day when I walked in the village. I remembered how the people glared at me with suspicious eyes and whispered behind my back. They had changed when I hadn't, and their human minds couldn't reconcile the majesty of my power. I feared that Aizel was right—that we would eventually have to leave this place for other lands.

"I feel it's the only way we're going to stay safe," she said, answering my thoughts. I did not scold her for fishing around in my head.

"And Blodwyn? Are you just forgetting about her?"

She shook her head. "No. But Blodwyn is not my path. You know I loved her just as much as you, but I have other things that are pressing to me. Constructing the necklace, perfecting my alchemy..."

"The books?" I interrupted.

"Yes, drafting the books. It needs to be done. And as an Aevir, with unlimited time, well…"

"And our time will expire when we've attained our goals?"

"I suspect so."

I took her words in, digested them. "But not now. Not right this moment, right?" I inquired, but the tone of my voice sounded more like a plea. A desperate plea to prevent the inevitable.

"No. Not right now, but soon."

"Where will we go?"

"Not *we*, Trond. We can't go together. We will have to part ways."

I nodded in agreement. She was right. It was the only way that made sense. If there were hateful people set out to destroy us, it would make sense to be apart. It would also make sense to stay together as a united front, but what did I know…

"You would grow bored. Restless. The body of a young woman, I possess. But the mind and wisdom of a crone are at the center of my core. I no longer desire you, Trond. I have no more passion inside. I think we've both known that for a while now. But it doesn't mean I love you any less; in fact, I love you more than you can understand. You are still a young man—handsome, dashing, charming, virile. And I know you will bring Blodwyn back. You will make your mother proud. You will make me proud." She reached in and kissed me gently on the cheek. It stung my flesh.

"Words of fire," I muttered and smiled.

"Runes of the elders," she replied.

"Only you, Aizel. Only you."

"I hate that name," she scoffed, bringing levity to our moment. "I've always hated it."

"We'll both have to change our names, I suppose," I said. "Why don't you just re-arrange the letters of yours? Reinvent what's already there."

She smirked and nodded. "I like that idea. I look forward to the day I am no longer Aizel Olz, but *still* Aizel Olz."

I kissed the top of her head gently. "This isn't goodbye, yet."

She sighed heavily. "No, not yet."

"And we will meet again."

"Amidst the paper-thin cry of the locust," she sighed again, and we embraced for what felt like another lifetime.

Part 2

Chapter Seven

Wednesday, May 25th 1966
Trent's Apartment
Crescent City Café
San Francisco, California
Night of the Waxing Crescent Moon

I lived in a cycle of centuries. Sixty to eighty years of being a member of society in some capacity, and twenty to forty years of rest. I had been told that I rested in my mother's womb for seventeen years before I finally made my appearance into this world, so therefore, I adopted that tradition into my everyday life. I figured since I was destined to live for an infinite amount of time, I would need intervals to recharge, so to speak. So as a man, I lived as a man would—sixty, seventy, maybe eighty years. When that time was over, I would commit myself to a place of solace for some time before I reawakened and was "reborn" so to speak. Underground, abandoned cemeteries, churches, the old cave in the north— one would be surprised at how many places there are in this world that remain untouched or forgotten. The slumber was always good for me. It allowed me to regroup, change over, build back my strength and energy. And every time I rose, the world had changed ever-so-slightly, yet the people proved to always stay the same. In all my years walking this planet, I had witnessed all types of revolutions and changes and shifts in society that indicated the evolution (or in some cases, the de-evolution) of humanity.

Oh, the sights that I have seen!

Through the course of the centuries, my plans altered—with the changing times, with my changing mind. By the 1400s, I no longer sought to resurrect Blodwyn in the traditional "bring-your-body-back-to-life" way. For I had learned so much in my time spent on Earth, and I had gained so much more power that I came to understand that her physical body was not necessary for the overall culmination of things. It was her spirit that was needed. The manifestation of what was left of her essence in the cosmos.

I spent most of the 1600s tracking that manifestation down until I found the source in a small town in Massachusetts. That was where I met Barbara—a powerful heksa with the soul and spirit of Blodwyn. But she wasn't Blodwyn. But she was. Regardless, Barbara was the Blodheksa—and she brought forth the twins, the Blodbrødre and Blodsøster. With Aizel (also known as Eliza "Goody" Olson) by our side, we were closer to bringing forth the New Eden than we had ever been in the past. But alas...

I thought of Barbara every day and was confident our paths would cross again eventually.

After a long rest at the end of the 1800s, I awoke again after the turn of the 20th century, unprepared for what was to come. The changes in society, the advancements in technology—it all seemed to ramp up at a breakneck pace, more than any other decade or century from the past. Truly, a far cry from the old ways of the colonial era. And at the center of it all, at the very heart of progression and advancement and new ways of thinking, was none other than America. It was the place to be! It was new and exciting and building up so quickly that one could scarcely keep up with it all. I was thankful I had an unlimited amount of time to experience everything—so much so that in 1960, when I had planned on committing myself to my traditional slumber, I couldn't bring myself to do it. I had to stay awake. I had to witness what was going to happen next.

Chapter Seven

The 1960s was an interesting time. Underneath the peace, love, and happiness, a counterculture was brewing. One that breathed shadows and menace. It reminded me of the insanity that befell the poor men and women during the Salem and New Haven Harbor witch debacle or the taboo mystique of the Gentry Brothers Wonders of the World carnival lifestyle in the mid-west. But this was different. This time, I felt that monsters like me could hide in plain sight, and I wasn't wrong. Something drew me in like a magnet. Guided by my dreams, I went as far west as west could go—California.

Nights in San Francisco were spectacular—especially in 1966, and especially on Folsom Street. There was nightlife that felt like its own living, breathing entity, and I was drawn to the energy that thumped like a heartbeat when the sun went down.

And while society was once again shifting in its collective thoughts and beliefs, I was still on the hunt for the Blodheksa— the one true witch who could bring about the new world. How I had longed for that day for over a millennium! With so many close calls over the centuries, and so many potential candidates, I knew the hour was at hand. By that time, my influence had spread far and wide, and I was certain all the pieces were suddenly moving to my side. It was palpable— especially in California.

I dreamed of California. It was a song stuck in my head. It was an image behind my closed eyes. It was a red-headed witch with the power to expel babies from wombs and demons from souls. It was a black-headed witch with a jealous smile plotting to usurp power for her own devices. It was a white-headed witch with black tattoos of the ancient symbols running up and down her arms standing at the edge of hell commanding the legions of creatures to devour the infidels of this mortal coil.

My sister was the most powerful heksa I'd ever known.

And if just the thought of California filled me with such emotion, there was no denying the fact that I needed to be there.

A dark shadow blanketed the section of Folsom Street in downtown San Francisco like an invisible storm cloud looming overhead. The masses were oblivious to it, but my preternatural eyes could see. It was brightest at night. Sometimes, there were rips in the sky that formed without any involvement from me. Like they were created by a power unaware of the energy it wielded. They were like tiny eyes spontaneously blinking open with a dark, uncontrolled magic. I was perplexed at the randomness of it—the pockets of power-punched, pin-prick holes in the sky and the faint growls and moans from within begged to be released—begged to be set upon this Earth to do what they were always meant to do. I heard them all, and I tried to match their energy, tried to widen the portals and drag them through, but I knew in my heart that would be impossible to do. "Rest easy, sweet brethren," I would say in my thoughts. "Soon enough. Soon enough." There was no doubt something was happening here. There was someone out there with distinct abilities, and it was plain to see they were unaware of this power. I was determined to locate the source, make a connection, and further my work.

I stayed in a studio apartment above the Crescent City Café, a little eclectic coffee house on Folsom. It was relatively quiet during the day, but at night, it became a hub for poets and dreamers and those who railed against the "man." The last of the beatniks gave way to the hippie culture, yet everyone gathered at Crescent City to bond and share and "be cool." Everything was cool. It was *all* so very cool with its red velvet couches, mosaic tiled circular tables, candlelit wall sconces, beaded curtains adorning the walls, and of course the stage at the front window for the poetry readings and artistic performances. The owners had tried to recreate the feel of old New Orleans and blend it with the contemporary vibe of Folsom Street. For being a coffee house, the actual coffee took a backseat to the pulsating culture. Regardless, they took me on as their personal handyman. They didn't pay much, but the lodging was free to make up for the piss-poor salary. Not the most glamorous position I'd held through the years but certainly not the worst. It was a fairly easy gig that allowed me much freedom.

The night was clear, and the crescent moon smiled at me from my casement window. The café below had begun to come to life as someone had taken to the stage to begin the nightly performances. I sat down on my couch expecting the usual rotation of bongo drums, finger snaps, and stream-of-consciousness prose to entertain me that evening. Even though it was all muffled through the thin walls, I could still hear and envision the performances in my mind's eye. Sometimes they were awful, sometimes they were mildly entertaining, but I listened and enjoyed all the same. I would rather be in the comfort of my cramped space than in the thick of the crowd anyway.

The first artist tapped loudly on the microphone, and the crowd laughed when the feedback from the amp filled the room with a high-pitched screech. I smiled to myself because this seemed to be the norm for the first presenter of the night. It was the running joke amongst the café's "usuals" that the first to go was the first to blow out everyone's eardrums.

The man cleared his throat with a deep booming sound coming over the microphone, and the crowd settled down. "In Nomine Dei Nostri Satanas, Lucifer Excelsi," he said with a clear, strong voice that had reached me in my apartment without any distortion.

I froze up for a second. Not only had the voice reached me undisturbed from the drywall, but there was something about it, something familiar to it. The voice had a musical tone to it—guttural, ancient. It lilted up from the floorboards and filled my room with a soothing sound. Silence deafened the entire space below, as if the people in the café had been lulled into a trance. The hairs on my arms stood up, and a chill raced through me. I thought, "Did they all hear the song, too?"

"In the Name of Satan, Ruler of the Earth, I invite the Forces of Hell to bestow their great power upon us this year, 1966, the year of our Lord, year one. Anno Satanas," the speaker declared.

My interest was more than piqued. Music filled my head and voices from somewhere deep in my soul seemed to sing out. A longing in my heart swelled to a crescendo, and before I could listen to any more from the confines of my room, I exited and trotted down the stairs to the back door that connected the café to the above apartments.

Just as I had envisioned, the café was silent and motion-less—as if everyone was frozen in place with drinks in hand and eyes fixed on the man at the small stage. Clad in black from head to toe, his long, stringy hair hung over his eyes and down to his shoulders. His gaze met mine when I came clamoring through the back door, yet no one else in the room seemed to notice my entrance as not a single head swiveled in my direction.

He reached into his back pocket, removed a piece of paper, and unfolded it. "Out of the Darkness," he began to read. "We are but flies flitting out of the darkness swarming to the rotted meat of the boar's head on a stick. We are but an island of loneliness, fighting for the survival of our souls. We are but a mere speck of sand on the beach washed away by the angry shores. But together, to break the system, to fill the land with dunes and rocks, we are legion. Together in his name, in *our* names we rise above the system trying to bring us down. For we can come out of the darkness and cast our shadows over the world."

He folded up the paper and jammed it back into his pocket. The people in the café raised their hands and voices in applause. *Someone read* Lord of the Flies *one too many times,* I think as he gave a small smile and slithered down the steps of the stage and over to one of the empty tables in the back of the room. The next performer skipped up to the mic and rattled a tambourine. The audience was enthralled with her display and swayed back and forth when she started reciting a poem from memory to go along with the music.

But I didn't hear a tambourine. I heard a drum. It was a low sound as if it was beating far off in the distance, playing just for me. Yet, the steady sound grew louder as the man from the stage got closer. I watched him intently as he sat down and scanned the room, darting his eyes back and forth and all around like he was looking for someone, or waiting for someone to enter and join him at his table. It was obvious he was avoiding eye contact with me. He purposefully would look straight ahead, but his peripheral caught my stare. Pina, the owner of the café came over to him and asked if he wanted a cappuccino, but he shook his head and waved her away.

A familiar shift in the atmosphere trailed the motion of his hands, and I immediately tensed up. Intrigued. Confused. I had only seen other heksas exude energy like that, yet I had felt nothing unnatural about the young man. My preternatural senses had not alerted me that he was anything more than a normal man around twenty years of age.

I took a step closer to his table and heard Pina say, "You did great up there," over the furious rattle of the tambourine, to which he nodded a thank you and smiled and waved his hand in the air again that sent her on her way.

She swished passed me, and her broomstick mesh skirt brushed against my leg. "Two," I said to her, holding up two fingers.

She nodded and flitted to the back kitchen.

The drumbeat in my head quickened as the roar of the café's cheers for tambourine girl died down. An intense need to know who the young man was ate away at me, and every second Pina took with my cappuccino order was maddening. When she finally came back, I fished in my jeans pocket for money, but she drove her elbow into my side and gave me a wink. "Your landlady will add it to your tab," she joked because she *was* my landlady.

"Thank you," I said with a fake smile.

I walked over to the table, set the cup of cappuccino in front of the stranger, and took the seat across from him. He furrowed his eyebrows angrily and looked me up and down.

"Pina is the owner and the landlord. She said any friends of mine…"

"Excuse me?" he spat in his deep voice. "I don't know you."

I ignored his reaction. "I live upstairs so I come down here a lot to watch the performances. I haven't seen you in here before."

He sucked in his teeth and took his elbows off the table defensively. The candlelight in the room danced off his face, and I struggled to make out his features from behind his shaggy hair. "First time here," he grunted. "I just wanted to check it out and read my work."

I tried to keep it light and unassuming. "Oh," I feigned surprise. "When you looked at me before I thought that…"

He eyed the cup in front of him then stared me down. "You thought wrong."

I shifted in the chair, pulling it closer to the edge of the table. I couldn't help but smile at his assumption I was hitting on him. I shook my head at his reply. "Your poem," I said nodding my head in his direction. "It was deep."

He looked away and back out into the crowd as if he didn't acknowledge what I was saying, as if he was still looking for someone. "Yeah," he muttered.

I leaned in closer and caught his attention, and when he looked at me, I locked my eyes with his. In mine, a red flame danced wildly, burning an entire city to the ground. I held his gaze and made him watch the fire until it burned out and my eyes turned back to gray. He squirmed a little when he saw it and his brows raised in disbelief. "Uhh… uhh…" he stuttered, a marked change from his indifferent tone toward me earlier.

"The invocation," I said quietly. "I was especially intrigued by it. What did you mean by 'the year of our Lord, year one'?"

The young man continued to stare, still baffled by the display in my eyes.

"How rude of me," I said, extending my hand to shake his. "I'm Trent, and I'd like to hear more about your work."

The man shook his head and snapped out of his trance. "Chris," he responded and reluctantly reached for my hand. When I took his in mine, a surge of energy raced up my arm. It was faint, but it was there, and it confirmed what I had originally felt: he had no knowledge of what resided in him. There was a dormant energy within, and I was even more interested to probe deeper.

"So, Chris," I continued, "tell me about that poem."

Tell me all about your power.

Chris darted his head around the room to see if anyone in the immediate vicinity was listening or watching and snaked in closer to me. "Year one," he said in a hushed voice. "Anno Satanas."

"The year of Satan."

"Our Lord and Master!" Chris quietly exclaimed.

"Out of the Darkness," I repeated the title of his poem. "It had power to it. The message about legion was very clear.

It seems our interests might be aligned because I know that power. I'm very interested in power like that. There are certain people who have an energy to control it and use it to do their will. Do you know what I mean?"

"Fuck yeah!"

"I'm looking for like-minded people like myself to work on a little something I've been, for lack of a better word—conjuring—for a little while now."

He paused again and looked over his shoulder. "Have you heard of Dr. Anton LaVey?" he asked quietly.

I narrowed my eyes.

"He is Mephistopheles incarnate. A brilliant man. On Walpurgisnacht last month he officially created the Church of Satan. Over on California Street. The Black House. The power you're talking about is at that house, ya know. Groovy stuff. LaVey is our Father in Black, and when he preaches, it's like nothing you've ever seen, man." He looked over his shoulder again suspiciously.

"The Black House?" I inquired.

"He has big plans. Ceremonies. Baptisms. Weddings. Rituals. He'll ordain priests and priestesses. A coven of witches…"

"On California Street?" I interrupted.

"Yeah, yeah. California Street."

I realized that wasn't far from Folsom and could possibly be the reason why I had been feeling all the energy lately. Chris certainly had something going on with him, as well, and now my focus and attention were centered on this newly formed Church. If I was intrigued before…

"I want in," I said with finality. "I would really like to meet the High Priest. LaVey, you said his name was?"

At the sound of LaVey's name, Chris shot back in his chair and his expression darkened. "Man, I don't know. I don't know you or anything, and…"

"Sure, you do," I replied jovially. "You know me now. And I know you saw…"

A faraway glaze came over Chris's eyes. Even with the energy inside him, he was still easily manipulated.

Even so, he hesitated. "Let me talk to my people. You know the little club down the street from here? The one tucked away far from the road?"

"The Inferno Club?"

"Yeah. Meet me there Friday night." He looked around the room again and spotted a young woman with medium-length brown hair. He stood up and gave her a head nod.

So, he was *waiting on someone.*

"Okay," I replied and finally took a sip of my drink.

"Yeah, gotta go now. My friend just got here." He was so distracted by the arrival of the woman that he didn't even look back at me. "But yeah, Friday. Nine o'clock. Inferno Club."

"Sure," I said, but he had already walked away.

Chapter Eight

Friday, May 27th 1966
The Inferno Club
San Francisco, California
Night of the Half Moon

I had been contemplative the two nights after my meeting with the so-called Satanist. In my mind, I had outlined all the possibilities and scenarios of just exactly what an organized Church of Satan meant because, with every religious sect and cult I had come across, pretenders and false prophets ran rampant. I had witnessed it time and time again in every aspect of life. But every so often, every once in a while, there was someone real and pure with an aligned intention and the ability to execute it. I concluded that it was the formation of this church that drew me to San Francisco in the first place and that I was intended to meet the head of it all, Dr. Anton LaVey, to determine if there was a Blodheksa in his flock of dark sheep.

The Inferno Club was exactly as Chris said—a hole in the wall. Located in the back section of a wicker furniture store off Folsom, The Inferno Club was hidden away from the rest of the district—a place for deviants and drug dealers and gamblers and mob types to come in and conduct business away from the prying eyes of the innocent and unknowing tourists.

A wave of smoke stung my eyes when I walked in, and the haunting beat of the Rolling Stones' "Paint it Black" filled my ears. People sandwiched shoulder to shoulder near the pool table and jukebox—hard-looking, leather-clad types who rode motorcycles and drank bourbon. A topless girl gyrated in an oversized birdcage that was on a raised platform behind the bar. She mouthed the lyrics to the song as she clutched one of her exposed breasts, spread her legs, and bent her knees in a suggestive way. I arrived at ten of nine, and to my surprise, Chris was already there drinking at the bar and watching the dancer. He gave me a sideways glance when I took the seat next to him. He downed the last of whatever was in his glass. "Hey," he exhaled, slamming it on the bar top.

"Whatcha drinkin'?" I asked.

He jutted his chin at his empty glass. "Jack."

I gestured for the bartender, who came over with another glass, filled it for me, and refilled Chris's. We held our glasses up and sipped at the same time. "So, what's the good word?" I inquired.

Chris looked at me sharply with a stern face, jumped up from the barstool, and hurriedly walked to an empty table in the corner of the room. I picked up my whiskey and followed. "Dude, keep it down!" he admonished.

I looked around, confused. "Huh?"

He pushed his long hair back from his face revealing his large brown eyes to me. They were anxious and nervous eyes. Suspicious eyes. Eyes that had seen things but couldn't understand what they were. Eyes that had wanted to believe what they had seen but couldn't rectify or justify or clarify the images with his brain. Eyes that had wanted to see the truth, but whose heart was still too afraid to acknowledge the wonders that encompass the universe. I sighed at this revelation. He was so young—a baby soul of sorts, and I knew his power would never be fully realized. He was too married to the mortal coil to see the beyond in its full glory. With the right guidance and training, he could have been something great.

If only you knew the power that's inside you…

Chris continued to fidget, and like the other night, he began scanning the room as if looking for someone. "So, what's your deal, man?" he finally said after he finished his drink.

"You tell me. I'm intrigued by the church you speak of. I told you, I want in. I think I have a lot to contribute, and I'm interested in helping to get the word out. Ya know, getting the organization off the ground, so to speak."

He hesitated. "Yeah, but they don't know you, and they're a little skittish about new people…"

"But it's a church, right? Don't they *want* new recruits? You can vouch for me."

He squirmed again. "Yeah, sure. I mean, I guess."

"Isn't that what they have you for? To go forth and spread the dark word? You're supposed to bring in people like me, right?"

"Right. I guess you can come to a service and all…"

I wagged my forefinger back and forth. "Yeah. No. That's all good and well, but I really need to see your top guy."

Because I have a book he might be interested in…

Chris froze and stared. I knew he heard me on the inside, but his suspicious and unbelieving mind had chalked it up to the alcohol talking. He blinked rapidly a few times trying to purge my voice from his head.

I tempered myself and took in a breath, calming down so I could lay everything out rationally for the youngling. "Like I told you the other night—I've been working on something. Research. I've been a student of the occult for a long time, and I think I have some information that could be useful to the cause. But it must be LaVey. I can't go through any of his underlings or lower-level people."

Aizel's life work was at my disposal. I held in my possession one of the six completed Blodheksa books—the books she crafted by hand and spirit and soul and mind and body and blood. She had cloaked them with her dark magic so that only someone of true heksa ilk could have the words revealed to them. I was tempted to invite Chris back to my apartment to show him and awaken the voice I knew lingered in his soul. But that would be awfully premature on my part. He truly was but a youngling. However, LaVey was a different story. I had dug around some, gotten some word from the street, and the consensus seemed to be that Dr. Anton was the *man*. The head honcho. "A"-number-fucking-one. If I could get the book to him, together we could

Chris raised his eyebrows. "What type of research?"

"There's an invocation," I said out loud. *To open the gates.* "But there are a lot of aspects involved." *And the world will be new again.* "And who better to review my findings than the man himself? If he's everything you say he is…"

"Oh, he is!" Chris exclaimed defensively.

"So, help me set this meeting up," I implored. "You seemed so gung-ho about your ministry the other night when we talked about it at the café. Why are you so cagey about it all of a sudden?"

Chris opened his mouth to reply, but before any words could come out, my stomach sank like a stone, and a young woman trotted over to our table. She was fully dressed now, but I realized she was the topless dancer in the cage, and the girl Chris had been waiting on the other night at the café. Something radiated from her like some type of forcefield. Like putting two opposite sides of a magnet together—there's a push-and-pull energy that makes you want to smash the magnets together because you're determined to force them together, but you also want to pull them away all at the same time. When she slid up behind Chris and wrapped her arms around his shoulders, her energy sucked him in—drew his low-burning fire into her magnet field and fed off whatever dormant power he had inside. It swirled like a red twister around their connected bodies. I don't even think she realized she did it, but when his shoulders slouched forward slightly as part of his spirit left him, and her chest puffed up with the essence that she stole, I knew he was gone, and our conversation was over.

Her shaggy brown hair covered his face as she whispered something in his ear.

"Yeah, I'm ready," he said in reply, and as she threw her head back to disengage from her embrace, a red X flashed on her forehead for me. I did a doubletake and clenched my glass.

Chris stood up. "Thanks for the drink."

I nodded. "Sure. Just think about what I said."

The young woman stepped away and held her arm out behind her to lead Chris out of the club. He grabbed her hand and followed. "I will definitely pass it along," he said over his shoulder.

I finished my drink as I watched them walk out together. I was defeated. I knew I had to figure out a better way to get an audience with the Dark Priest because there was *something* to all of this. I had been called here specifically—just like I had been called to all the other places throughout my long life – and my gut was telling me I was close to carrying out my purpose.

"Why so glum, chum?" A bell-like voice broke me from my thoughts. One of the waitresses from the club stood beside me with a cocktail tray in hand. I barely noticed her face or what she was wearing, but there was something in her voice that was soothing to my ears and caused me to smile. "Can I get you another?"

"No. No. I'm good," I said and waved my hand in the air.

She bent over and grabbed my empty glass from the table. "Okie dokie," she sang.

My heart stopped when her necklace dangled in front of my face. It glittered and glinted in the darkness, and the air left my lungs. I think I gasped. No, I know I did. I gasped. Hard and loud. I thought my eyes had deceived me, but as she pulled away there was no question about it—it was the pendant—Aizel's pendant. It swung from a new silver chain and was finely polished with a substance that made it smell of unnatural chemicals, but I knew what it was. I knew it was the real deal. I knew it was the ancient container of a draugr. I felt it. I heard it—like it was laughing at me from within the depths of its confinement. The last time I had seen it or touched it was over two-hundred years ago. Lifetimes ago. See, Aizel had completed her life's work, and by 1695, she passed on. I had assumed the pendant was lost around the same time.

But here it was. An ancient relic belonging to my brethren flung about the neck of a modern-day bar waitress. The questions bombarded my thoughts all at once: How did it come to

be in her possession? How did she get it? And, most importantly, how was she still alive after wearing it?

Unless...

"You okay there, Daddy-o?" she asked in a concerned tone,
snapping me from my jumbled thoughts.

I swiveled my head to look at her. "Fine, fine," I lied.
Because I most definitely was *not* fine, but I tried to play it off
like everything was cool.

She proceeded to wipe up the table with a white rag.
"Sure," she drawled sarcastically. "Your buddy totally ditched
you for Susan. I get it. I'duh ditched you for her, too."

"Oh yeah?" I said inquisitively. "She's not all that
hot, though."

She smiled and sighed. "Yeah, well, Susan's got something
about her that makes the boys go wild. That Atkins girl is
gonna go places."

I grabbed her slender wrist gently and she stopped and
gazed into my eyes. I held her there, trying to figure out the
whos and whats and whys and hows. Her skin was pale and
soft like flower petals, but her eyes were black and wide,
and deeply set into her face to where her cheeks jutted out
sharply around them and were framed by her black hair bob
cut. The necklace rested perfectly against the visible bones of
her rail-thin chest, and I couldn't help but think she looked
like someone I once knew. "You'll go places, too," I said.
"Anywhere you want."

She rolled her eyes and turned from me. "Oh yeah,
Daddy-o? I suppose you're the one who's gonna take me
there? Get me out of this shithole city, wife me up, and make
an honest woman out of me? Oh, no wait," she clucked,
"you're gonna make me a movie star! Get me in front of all
those cameras. I'll be the next Marilyn! Puh-leez. Save your
schtick. Nothing I haven't heard before."

I gave her a side smirk. "Wow. You're a little hellflower
aren't you? If I didn't know any better, I'd say you were
flirting with me!" I teased.

She chuckled. "Oh no, Daddy-o, definitely the other way
around!" I could tell she was smiling, but my eyes were fixed

on the pendant. I was determined to find out more. "Can I get you anything else?"

"Your time?" I said, turning up the charm. "Sit down with me for a little bit, ya know, being that my friend ditched me for a hottie and all..."

Her eyes grew wide with indignation, and she put one hand on her hip. "Hey!" she exclaimed. "You said..."

"Susan ain't got nothing on you, darling."

'Cause yes, Susan is going places, just not the places you think...

Her body relaxed and her face softened at my flattery, but still, my eyes were trained on the necklace. A light around it twinkled and swelled and mesmerized me to the point that I couldn't tell which I was interested in more—the girl or the jewelry.

I pulled out the chair next to me.

"I'm not 'darling,'" she huffed. "I'm Poppy. And I can't. I'm still on shift."

"Well, you literally *are* a little hellflower! And I'm not Daddy-o. I'm Trent."

"Like I said, Trent. I'm still on shift. Maybe some other time. So, other than the honor of my company, which is off the menu, what can I get ya?"

"A Coke. Just a Coke."

For the rest of the night, I watched Poppy flitter about the club delivering drinks to the patrons, cashing out tabs, smiling brightly at anyone who stuffed a few dollar bills down her low-cut shirt. Occasionally she would bring me another Coke, and we would continue our playful banter. At one point she said, "Don't you have to pee by now?" It hadn't even registered to use the bathroom, so I got up and did. By the time I got back, Poppy was topless in the cage, grinding her body to the beat of a Jimi Hendrix song. But we locked eyes, and I took all of her in—danced with her in her mind's eye, beckoned her to me. Barely a woman's shape to her, her small breasts were like nubs protruding from the bones of her chest. And every bone of her ribcage was pressed tightly against her pale skin, giving her an eerie skeletal look as she danced around the cage. Skin and bones, and yet I needed to have her. Needed to take her to my secret space in the woods. Needed to run my hands over her flesh and be engulfed in the power of the necklace once again.

When her performance was over, she went to one of the backrooms, got dressed, and cashed herself out for the night. It was 2:00 a.m., and I had drunk about all the Coke I could possibly fathom. *Enough for one lifetime, that's for sure.* She breezed passed me at the bar pretending not to notice I was there. Quickly, I reached out my arm and caught her shoulder. She whipped around with a mock look of surprise on her face. "Oh, you're still here?"

"I figured you could use an escort home. Ya know, it being late and all, and this being a shithole city. It's not safe for you to be out there alone."

She smirked and her eyebrows disappeared under her black bangs. "Oh, really? You're going to drive me home, Daddy-o?"

"No ma'am," I shot back. "But you knew that, didn't you."

She chuckled. "Maybe." Then, she leaned in forward and gave me a playful swat on my arm. "Kidding!" she relented with another laugh. "Funny thing is, I don't need an escort home. I live right upstairs, so I guess you hung around for nothing."

I tilted my head down and gave her a knowing glare.

She shifted uncomfortably for a second. "But *you* knew *that*," she said with disbelief.

"C'mon," I said cheerfully, trying to ease her anxiety. "How would I know that? That's impossible."

"I don't know. Sometimes people know things."

"This is true. But I will say this—I *do* know that beautiful young women shouldn't walk home alone this late at night regardless of how near or far their home is."

She thought about my words, as the full effects of my charm covered her like a warm and comforting blanket. "How do I know you're not the Boston Strangler or something?"

"They caught him already."

"Well, then how do I know you're not the Folsom Street Strangler?" she teased.

"Only if that's who you want me to be," I taunted back seductively.

Her small pink tongue darted across her lips. "Okay, Daddy. You can escort me up the two flights of stairs. Then I'll let you know if I still feel safe or not."

"Fair enough, Hellflower. Fair enough."

Chapter Nine

Saturday, May 28th 1966
Poppy's Apartment
Above The Inferno Club
San Francisco, California
Morning of the Waxing Gibbous Moon

Rays of the morning sunlight struggled to make their
way through the cracks of the blinds in Poppy's apartment. The gray haze of the San Francisco morning prevented
them from beaming full force with all their shimmering glory,
which was fine by me—I needed to sleep. After the last few
laborious hours spent in the throes of unbridled passion, and
the mystery of Aizel's ancient necklace weighing heavily on
my consciousness, I found myself weary in both body, spirit,
and mind. Poppy's scrawny frame rested against me, deep
in a dreamless sleep. She nestled her head in the crook of
my arm and curled up one leg over my chest as I wrapped
my arm around her shoulder. I wasn't comfortable with her
resting on me for she wasn't soft and silky like other women I
had known. Her body was stiff and hard—the bones that pro-
truded from her thin skin were like stabbing knives shooting
out from her neck and hips and shoulder and ankle. I was
afraid to touch her at first—afraid to break her frail structure. When I railed into her and the bones of her pelvis jabbed

into my stomach, I had to stop for a second and make sure I didn't crack her like a wishbone. It was the same thing, too, when I took her from behind and the bones of her ass-cheeks poked at me. It felt so strange, and I couldn't determine if I liked it or not. It was like when someone says, "Eat this; it's gross!" so you try it, and one part of you is like "Yeah, I'm down with this," and the other part of you is like "Fuck, get it away from me!"

Well, that was Poppy for me. One taste was delicious, and one taste was repulsive—both at the same time.

And all throughout the wild and unfamiliar night of sex, the pendant lay peacefully on the nightstand next to the bed. There were so many missed opportunities to grab it and go, and I only had myself to blame. So, I was stuck there on the twin-sized bed—sandwiched between the bag of bones draped across me and the peeling blue paint of the stucco wall, the sun fighting against the gray sky of the morning and the noise of Folsom Street in full swing below. I stared at the popcorn-textured ceiling above me, thinking about my options and exit strategy.

Folsom Street wasn't the only thing waking up, though— Poppy stirred and shifted against me, and I quickly closed my eyes and pretended I was still asleep. Violently, she twisted her upper torso and reached for something on the nightstand. After a second, she muttered "Fuck!" jumped up from the bed and hurriedly scampered into the bathroom. When I heard the water pour out from the showerhead, I opened my eyes and rolled over to the nightstand. The dainty Omega watch read 11:00 a.m., and I was a little taken aback myself that it was so late in the morning.

But with Poppy out of sight, I had the perfect opportunity. A low rumble sound filled my ears and I breathed in. Blindly, my fingers danced across the surface of the nightstand, making contact with the cheap chain at first, then inching their way down to the prized possession. Instantly, a surge of heat raced into my fingers and spread into my palm. I clutched it tightly and brought it to my chest—holding it there, letting the power of it engulf me in a wave of magnetic energy. Once in its dome, the air shifted, and I saw a thousand stars in front of my eyes as the memories of my previous times with it flooded back to me. The draugr inside was still there. *Hello, old friend,* I thought in a hazy drunken-like stupor. *Remember me?* Music played in the energy dome—chants of the ancients, and a low-beating drum, and the voices of the old ones screaming in agony (or laughing in excitement, I couldn't tell). The power had only increased over the years, and I swooned at the overwhelming sensation of it all. It was glorious! For a split second, I wondered how Poppy was able to wear the necklace and not feel it or be affected by it, but a surge of heat shook the lower half of my body like an orgasm, and I quickly lost focus.

Suddenly, the room went dark and the stars around me shone brighter. An invisible hand lifted me from the bed, and I reached up to touch each and every star—tried to catch them all in my hands and keep them safe with me forever—but the sky ripped open and dripped with blood, so I opened my mouth to taste it. I rose higher and higher in the sky as each droplet entered my mouth and coated the back of my throat with its metallic flavor. Images of the past and present and future flashed like wild lightning in my head. Things that had happened, and things that were to come. The blood belonged to the Satanist called Chris—the young man with a dormant power. He tasted of burnt leaves strewn across a hunk of rotted meat. Every globule I ingested constructed the picture of his mangled face—a brown eye dangling from the socket, his tongue split down the center like a serpent and hanging from one side of his lifeless mouth. I was drunk on his foul blood. It sang to me the songs of the old ones in the language of my soul. Runes branded themselves onto his naked body with the edges of the burnt leaves, and I read the message clearly: "The young man's untapped power was wasted on him—and the old ones wanted it back…"

In an instant, I plopped back onto the bed with a thud, and before I had a moment to fully digest what I had seen, Poppy was in the doorway wrapped in a pink robe. She switched on the overhead light in the room. "What, the, actual, *fuck*, was, *that*?" she gasped in disbelief, with an emphasis on each word.

I clutched the pendant tighter in my palm as if to shield it from her—to protect it from her prying eyes.

She was flabbergasted. "Did you just... did I just see... what in the *fuck*, Trent?" There was something odd about the tone of her voice, though. Like she almost knew what was going on. Like she had known all along but had never actually witnessed it with her own eyes. Like the belief in something of long ago had finally manifested itself before her eyes and her brain was reconciling the deep-seated belief with the reality of it all.

"I don't know what you're talking about," I lied and sat up.

She placed her hand on her hip and bounced up and down on the ball of one foot. "Bull fucking shit, dude! I know what I saw! How the fuck did you do that?"

"Poppy, really, I..." I stammered like an asshole. She had taken me off guard, and I didn't have a prepared reaction.

"Well, fuck you!" she exclaimed. She bounced onto the bed next to me and grabbed at my wrists. I was still reeling from the swoon of Chris's blood, and when she jerked my hands, the pendant fell to the bed in the space between us. "My necklace?" she questioned excitedly. "Were you gonna rob me or something?"

"No, no, no! Nothing like that," I coaxed.

She held on to my wrists and stared at me for a few moments. Her pulse radiated fiercely from her fingertips, and in the bubble of space between the draugr and me, she soon steadied her breathing and relaxed. "Am I still dreaming? Am I still fucked up from last night?"

"You're awake," I said calmly. "You're awake, and we didn't get drunk last night."

"You know shit, don't you," she said with a serious tone. "Spooky shit. That guy you were talking to... he's been hanging around the club. Susan told me he's connected. You're one of them, aren't you?"

"No. I'm not one of *them*..."

She jolted her body on the bed and brought both her fists down playfully on my chest. "Why didn't you tell me!" she laughed. "I love spooky shit!"

I ignored her enthusiastic acknowledgment and jutted my chin to the necklace. "Where'd you get that?"

Poppy picked it up from the bed and dangled it in between us. My eyes followed it as it swayed back and forth and created a trail of stars in the empty space and mesmerized me with its power. Did she see it, too?

"This old, ugly thing? Looks like some kind of weird eye or something."

"It's not an eye," I said matter-of-factly. "It's a locust."

"Huh?"

"When a locust burrows deep in the ground, it stores all its energy, and when it emerges and is unleashed, it makes a wonderous sound for all to hear."

Her eyes widened with awe. "Wow!" she crowed. "I never looked at it that way. How did you know?"

I reached for the pendant and stopped it swaying in mid-air. "Where did you get it?" I repeated, ignoring her again.

"Oh, um… my grandmother. When she died, my mom and aunts paraded all the grandkids into her bedroom and put her jewelry box out. They told us we could each pick one item to remember her by. I picked this." She smiled.

"Why this? I'm sure she must have had other pieces."

She shrugged her shoulders. "I don't know. It was different. Weird. Like how I felt inside."

"Does *it* make you feel weird? Ya know, when you wear it?"

She tilted her head like a dog listening for a sound off in the distance. "Now that you mention it…" her voice trailed a little, "but I don't wear it often. Only sometimes when I work the club 'cause it's got that 'Inferno' vibe, I suppose. I don't know. Sometimes I feel lightheaded if that's what you mean."

I went silent. That explained why she hadn't been fully affected by it. The necklace was known to take human life if worn too often…

"Why? Do you know something? Like, about this?" She hurriedly sat up on her knees and bounced on the bed again. Her eyes sparkled with curious delight. "C'mon, Daddy-o! Talk to me!"

I knew I couldn't divulge the truth to her, but I also knew she wouldn't let up on the subject, so I resorted to a half-truth. "The necklace is a tool. Like the Ouija Board or Tarot Cards…"

"Can it conjure the dead?" she interrupted fervently.

"Hmmm… not in that way…"

"Can it be used to communicate with spirits?"

"I wouldn't say that…"

"What about spells? Can it make my wildest dreams come true? Can it make me become rich and famous? A Hollywood movie star with a giant mansion in the Hills, designer clothes, money at my disposal, and…"

"Slow down! Slow down!" I smiled at her innocent enthusiasm. "It's more like a glamouring."

Her nose crinkled up. "Huh? What's that?"

"A glamouring is like seeing something that isn't there. An illusion. A mirage…"

"A party trick!"

"Yes, Poppy. A party trick."

She placed the necklace next to my lap and clapped her hands together. "So, show me a cool trick, Trent!"

I furrowed my brow. "No, no. It doesn't work like that."

"Aww, c'mon," she pouted with her lower lip extended out with mock sadness. "Show me a spell. Pleeeeeeeaaaaaasssseee."

"How do you know I haven't already shown you one? How do you know you're not under one right now?"

'Cause you kinda are…

"Oh, please!" she huffed. "I'm a big girl. I can handle it. Show me something. Anything! I bet you show all your other girlfriends spooky shit."

I laughed. "Less than twenty-four hours and you're my girlfriend?"

"You know what I mean," she huffed again and rolled her eyes.

"No. I don't. Tell me what you mean," I said, trying to divert her attention from her need to see a spell.

"Now that we're together, I'm just saying, I have girlfriend rights. And I have a right to know what you know."

"Oh, Poppy," I sighed. "Those were other girls and other times."

She shimmied herself over my calves. "Look at you. With your dreamy gray eyes, modest build, charming and perfect smile, and California surfer-boy complexion. You know how devilishly handsome you are. I bet all the girls wanna fuck you. I'm sure your big dick helps in that department." She ran her hands up my bare thighs, stopping at my cock that quickened at her touch. "I bet you had a Wendy, and a Donna, and a Lisa, and a Carolyn, and a Jayne, and a Barbara..." My leg muscles quivered, and she paused to observe me quizzically. I gave no further indication of anything unusual or suspect, so she continued, "but I know damn straight you've never had a Poppy." With that, she seductively opened up the bottom part of her bathrobe to reveal a peak of her freshly shaved sex.

"You think you know everything?" I asked coyly.

"I know men. And I know you..." she whispered as she moved up, widened her legs, and plunged her opening onto my fully erect organ.

Swiftly, I put my hands underneath her robe and in one fell swoop, flung it off her shoulders and onto the bed. The heat of her sex engulfed me, but I wanted more. Needed more. The necklace was on the bed, and as she thrashed her boney self up and down on my shaft, I reached for it, and with both hands looped it over her head. I blinked a few times. The last name Poppy had said was Barbara, and the memories of her came flooding back...

I had a Barbara once. A long time ago, in a place on the opposite side of the world, I had a Barbara. A woman like no other. We were together once, in unholy matrimony. She bore my children. She bathed me in blood. She was Blodwyn reincarnate, yet her own divine being. And when we were together, the world stopped. Time stopped. The gash in the sky would tear wide open so we could both see through the here and now. When I mounted her, it was as if I had mounted a goddess with stars on her flesh and the old ones in her eyes — and we were one, and I consumed her, and she consumed me. And I made her an Aevir so that she and I could complete our life's work together even though we had been apart for hundreds of years.

I blinked my eyes, and Poppy was gone. In her place was Barbara riding me heartily, hungrily. Barbara in the flesh with her deft breasts and sweat-sheared skin. Soft and supple

Barbara, moaning my name and taking my full width and girth deep inside her. I reached up and grabbed onto the pendant, trying to hold on to her—to savor that moment, that memory, that *glamour*... Her long brown hair tossed about her shoulders, and her body moved so gently, yet with such purpose, that I couldn't help but come fast and hard—emptying everything I had deep into her loins.

I cried out when I came to completion. Poppy quickly disengaged and removed the necklace. Her skeletal body looked hazy at first, but slowly, it manifested back into view. Barbara was gone for now, but I was satisfied enough with having her for but a few minutes.

Poppy reached behind her and grabbed for her robe. "Fuck you, Trent," she hissed and jumped from the bed, taking the necklace with her.

"What are you talking about?"

"I saw her. Your *Barbara.*"

"Again, what are you talking about?" I don't know why I asked because I already knew the answer. Poppy saw. The glamouring was so strong that she couldn't have *not* seen it.

"Tell me about her," she demanded as she leaned in the doorway. "Was she such a special chapter in your book?"

I sighed heavily. "More like a book of her own."

"Well, if you wanna keep fucking me, that can't happen again. No more of that necklace voodoo, okay?"

I nodded, but I knew I had no intention of making this thing with Poppy a *thing*.

"You're lucky I'm not that attached to you yet, cause that woulda made me super jealous."

"Why do you think I would want to make you jealous anyways?"

She sighed and folded her robe over, concealing her scrawny body. "Because you're a guy. And guys do stupid shit like that. I know you, Trent Black—if that's even your real name. I know you and the games guys like you play. And I know you and me ain't gonna end well."

"Jesus, Poppy Smith!" I exclaimed. "If *that's* even *your* real name! Who the fuck hurt you?"

"It is my real name. Says so on my birth certificate. And life hurt me. Just plain old life. Life hurt me so bad I don't think there's any more hurt left to be had. So, you can tell me all about your women, Trent. Even Barbara. Because I know you've never had a Poppy, and if you hang with me for a little while, I know I'll give you plenty of stories to tell your next girl." She shut the light in the bedroom. "You gotta go now. I have some stuff to take care of, but I'll see you at the club tonight. I'm dancing at nine. Don't be late."

Chapter Ten

Monday, June 6th 1966
Trent's Apartment
Above The Crescent City Café
San Francisco, California
Night of the Waning Gibbous Moon

This night had been forespoken for many years—the perceived evil of the six, six, six. Religious fanatics lined the streets begging people to repent their sins and lift up their transgressions to the Lord above so they could be saved on this day of judgment. It was always a time for dire omens and superstitions to appear. "God is Dead," so said Nietzsche and *The New York Times*, and in my wise and humble opinion, I don't think I very much disagreed. Because throughout all my years—throughout all my iterations and experiences with a six, six, six, this one in particular *felt* different. There was something in the air. Some kind of tingling energy running marathons on my skin all day long. Any normal person would have dismissed it as the unusually cold weather that day, but there was a shift in the air that rattled my senses.

Pina had worn a blue Afghan blanket when we worked in the café that morning and complained about the cold. "If this really was a day for the devil," she said with staunch Catholic conviction, "wouldn't it be hot?"

"I don't think the devil has a preference either way," I inserted.

"Well," she scoffed, "hell is below. Ya know, the fiery pits of hell, the Lake of *Fire?* I'm just saying, if this was really the end of days, we'd be feeling the heat for sure. It's barely 70 out there today!"

"But that's not normal either, is it?" I teased.

She paused and thought for a moment. "Maybe God is taking extra measures to keep the flames at bay." A large smile invaded her face at the thought of being saved by her God, and she shimmied the Afghan higher on her shoulders with a sense of confidence and authority.

I nodded and continued fixing the cappuccino machine.

And while Pina was correct to an extent—because a day is just a day—I couldn't shake that crawling feeling all morning. I assumed Dr. LaVey and his congregation must have something planned for this unholy day, but my inner radar went far beyond those notions. I had had zero luck with getting a connection into The Church of Satan. Chris had been cagey about the whole situation ever since we met—one day he was intent on getting me an audience with the higher-ups, the next he was locked up and unwilling to even discuss the Church. It was weird. And all my efforts of glamouring and persuasion proved temporary or fruitless. I suspected it had something to do with the sleeping giant of power that existed inside him. I was glad he had no clue about the true nature of his own capabilities—his dormant force had proven to be problematic for me. I could only imagine what it would be like had he reached full potential. I started to think that maybe the problem wasn't my inability to get Chris to get me into the Church, but rather Chris himself…

Anyway, the foreboding feeling I had all morning lasted well into the night. After work, I threw the window in my apartment living room open and hung my head out of the casement. A blast of cold air caught me in the throat. It was as if the breeze had come directly off the surface of the waning moon to choke me. She waned but was still nearly full. Only a sliver of darkness crested on her right side. For the most part, she was illuminated and bright and glorious, and as I nodded in her direction with reverence, she sent another frigid blast that made my eyes water. I laughed and ducked my head back into the room and gazed at the night sky from inside. Like spiders dancing on my arms, my skin bloomed with goosebumps as the moon smiled back at me. She watched. She listened. She knew. And she told me something deep in my soul with the voice of my brethren. It sang through the trees of the concrete jungle city, lilted in the air against the car strewn streets, blended with the sounds of both nature and man...

She is coming.

I closed my eyes and deeply inhaled, letting the song and air and noise and message fill me to the point of near ecstasy.

She is coming.

The words were so clear and crisp in my consciousness, and I had heard them so distinctly like I had never gotten a message like that before. In all my immortal years, it was this night, this moon, this city, this time that finally aligned in my head and my heart and my soul.

She is coming. And everything else will come with her.

Year One.

Anno Sanguis Pythonissam.

Year of the Blood Witch.

The apartment door flung open, and Poppy bounced into the living room. Her pleather mini-dress stuck to her pale skin with sweat, her black makeup smeared around her eyes, and the pendant rested perfectly on one of the visible bones of her chest. I envisioned her surprise as she left the blazing the heat of the Inferno Club only to be full-body smacked with a wave of cold air on this chilly night. But the mile-wide smile plastered on her sunken face showed she cared less about the weather and more about what was brewing on her lips.

"Busy night?" I asked half-heartedly.

"No," she answered, sauntering into the room and lighting a cigarette. "But that's expected for a Monday."

"So, you got something to tell me..."

"I do! I do!" she screeched and flopped down on the couch next to me, next to the open window. She puffed hard on her cigarette and exhaled over my shoulder as if to send the plume of smoke into the night air. "So," she began as she ashed the cigarette onto the hardwood floor, "Susan talked to some big-time photographer the other day. He's connected. Like, *connected*!" Her dark eyes widened as she emphasized the word. "He's gonna photograph her for a spread that will appear in multiple magazines. *Multiple*, Trent. Like, this is some serious, groovy shit."

"Wow," I said, feigning excitement. "Sounds amazing."

She took another long drag. "Oh, you don't even know!" she gushed, almost choking on the smoke. "That's not even the best part."

"What is the best part?" I encouraged, unenthusiastically.

"She invited me to go! She wants me to be a part of the shoot!" She jumped up from the couch and danced around in a circle. The smoke from the cigarette circled around her ceremoniously, engulfing her in a spell of her own excitement.

"She invited you to a photo shoot?"

She threw her body to the floor and draped herself dramatically over my knees. "Yes, Trent!" she yelled excitedly. "This is huge! This could be my big break!" She dreamily lifted the cigarette up to my lips offering me a drag, which I accepted.

"When? Where? How much?" I asked with my smoky exhale to her face.

"Apparently that guy Chris that she's been hanging around—you know Chris, you talk to him a lot, too. Well, he hooked it up. He's a member of that Church of Satan. Knows all the top people. Some big-time foreign photographer is coming to the Black House to do an exclusive," she squealed. "They want to do some kind of publicity thing for the organization. 'LaVey's Lustful Church' or something like that. Work the sexy angle to draw more people in, I guess. I don't know if they really do that sex stuff, but they want to make it look like it. Sex and Satan, 'cause apparently sex and Satan sells."

Say you love Satan…

I was riveted, to say the least. If this was true, if Poppy was going to be at the Black House promoting the organization, then it was possible I had my "in" —my proverbial foot in the door.

"When is the shoot? I can go with you. Be your bodyguard of sorts." I laughed at the joke. It was funny, but not funny at the same time.

"Friday night. But I don't know," she hesitated. "Susan said it's a raw shoot."

"What does that mean?"

"Okay," she said in a serious tone. She stiffened her back, took the last puff, and ground the nub of the cancer stick into the floor. "There's a ninety-nine percent chance I will be topless... naked." She winced in anticipation of my reaction.

"Okay," I said, my voice trailing with an "I-don't-see-an-issue" tone.

"You're okay with that?"

"Why wouldn't I be?"

"You're not jealous?"

"Poppy, you dance topless in a cage six nights a week. Why would I be jealous over some photographs? If I was the jealous type, I wouldn't..."

"Well, maybe I want you to be a little jealous!" she raved. "Cause a little jealousy would show me that you really liked me."

I blinked a few times at the insanity of her statement. Her mania swirled not only in her kaleidoscope eyes but also in the space between us, and I held up my palms to try to suck that energy in. Poor, lost Poppy with so many insecure layers to her. It almost made me sad to feel how broken she was on the inside.

When I didn't respond, she stamped her foot and turned away. "Fine!" she huffed. "You obviously don't care about my good news. I'm gonna go..."

"Stop!" I said, reaching for her. I couldn't let her go—not at that moment when the moon had sung, and Poppy had revealed her connection to LaVey, and the necklace hypnotized me, and the stars danced, and the six, six, six, and she is coming. She is coming. She is coming. She is... and a thought so delicious entered my mind, that I could barely stand it. A magical, mystical thought. A plan so wonderous, I wanted to punish myself for not dreaming of it sooner—like one hundred, two hundred, three hundred years sooner.

What if tonight was the night?

What if tonight was the night when the New Eden was to be born?

What if tonight was on my shoulders to open the gateway to the new world with the book, and the pendant, and the six, six, six...

"There's magic out there right now," I whispered. "Stay. We can celebrate."

Something resembling a smirk formed at the side of her lip, and as I led her into the bedroom, she relaxed her shoulders and calmed down.

"Take off your clothes," I instructed as I reached down under the bed and pulled out the book. My book. Aizel's book. The first and original one of six in the world.

"Oh," she groaned. "*That* kind of celebration."

"Not quite," I replied. "Just do it."

She stared at me, starry-eyed, and did as commanded. I removed my clothes, too, and I sat on the bed across from her, placing the book in between us.

"What's that?" she asked.

I inhaled with a knowing and peaceful deep breath. My personal, completed copy of *Blodheksa, Blodbrødre, og Blodsøster.* The runes within spoke loudly to me—filled my head with their stories and spells, begged me to open the pages and speak the words. The pentagram design on the front cover made me smile for it was the symbol of the heksas—my long line of powerful kin. "What do you see?"

"A book. A book, Trent. You just put a book on the bed."

"Yes, but what do you see?"

"There's a pentagram on the cover. Are you fucking with me right now?"

"What does the book say?" I pressed.

She picked it up, held it in front of her face, turned it all around in every direction and even fanned out the pages. The book hummed wildly to me when the pages were exposed, and I breathed in deeply again. A satisfying and fulfilling rush of air entered my lungs and set me with purpose.

She put the book back on the bed. "It's blank! Is this a trick?"

"So, all you see is the star on the cover, and nothing else? No writing, no title, no anything..."

"No. I told you it's blank. Just the star. Is this like a journal of yours or something?"

"Yes, Poppy, the story is yet to be written," I said, knowing full well the book was in fact complete. It must have been the power of the necklace that allowed her to see even that much. "Remember I told you about your necklace? How it's like a tool? Well, this book is another one of those tools."

"Oooohhh," she cooed. "Let me guess. You're gonna show me a spell!"

I reached across the space between us and motioned for the necklace. She leaned forward and allowed me to take it off her. "The necklace and the book can open the gate," I said. "There's something about tonight that just feels different. And if I'm right, you and I will open up the portal to all of our wildest dreams."

Poppy's eyes widened with fear and wonder. "You mean, I'm gonna be rich and famous?"

It took everything within me to keep from rolling my eyes. "Hmmm…," I mumbled, "not sure, but you're definitely going to be something."

Food for the old ones. A proper sacrifice.

We clasped hands over the book. "Close your eyes," I instructed, "and just relax. Be not afraid. I'm here with you. Whatever you see or hear, it's okay. I promise."

Poppy sucked in air like she was about to dive into a pool, then squeezed my hands tighter, pushing the metal of the locust pendant deep into my palm.

The room shifted. The density of the atmosphere weighed down on our chests causing our breathing to become more labored, and the color drained from my vision—no longer could I see in reds and greens and blues and yellows, but a sheen the color of aged paper fell over my line of sight giving everything an old golden tone. Poppy squirmed. She was uncomfortable in this transformed space, and I admonished her to keep her eyes closed.

"Who's Aizel? No, wait. Eliza. No, that's not right. Aizel. Eliza? I don't know…" she muttered.

"Shhhhh," I said. "Just go with it."

The book sang. The wrinkled and aged pages fanned out and spoke to me in the deepest part of my brain.

Poppy squeezed my hand harder. "There was a fire. They burned her. She screamed. And the babies? Oh God! The babies! Trent, is the apartment on fire? I smell smoke!"

"No. The apartment is not on fire. Trust me," I said gently, trying to calm her down. Her heart raced, and the sound of it beat against my skull. I heard the cries of the babies. I heard Aizel on the stake. 1696. Massachusetts. The aftermath of Salem. They finally killed her. She cried out for Blodwyn, and for Barbara, and for me...

"Trond? Who's Trond?" Poppy said. She heard it too. "Wait! No way! I don't... You? You? Who the actual fuck *are* you?" she screamed.

In her panic, she tried desperately to loosen her grip from me, but I pulled her in closer and harder, forcing her to stay. The metal of the insect pendant pierced through my skin and a thin line of blood trickled from my palm, through her fingers, and onto the book. A high-pitched hissing noise, like feedback from a stereo, filled both of our ears and made us both shudder. Poppy went limp and slumped forward onto the book—she had passed out from the images and sounds that had bombarded her mind.

My eyes began to come into focus. I noticed the room was intact, undisturbed, but the golden color had still clouded my vision. Poppy's face had landed in my lap, but surrounding her body was a circle of stars glittering like fairy dust in a magical forest. In the center of the circle, I saw through—like the rip in the sky to the other world, only this was to our world, just a view of another time. I had torn open a space in time, and could see right through to the other side...

The rider and his wife had been traveling for days. The horses were weary, and they were running out of supplies for the animals and themselves. If they didn't reach their destination soon, he was afraid he would have to sell a horse for sustenance or *use* a horse for sustenance. Either way was not an ideal situation. Liam was too proud to admit that he was lost—that he had lost his way in the forest miles and miles ago. But at what point would his pride cost him the life of his new bride, Colleen, or even his own? Besides, it had taken much maneuvering on his part to even get to Massachusetts. The Irish were often only brought over to America as indentured servants, so when Liam and Colleen O'Sullivan got on the ship out of England as John and Mary Smith, they were already determined to erase themselves and start anew. But if they didn't make progress and find the town they had planned to settle in, all hope would be lost, and all would have been for naught.

Smoke filled the air and Liam jerked on the horses' reins. "Whoa, whoa!" he called and surveyed the land around him with a furrowed brow. He took a makeshift map from his pocket, looked at it quizzically, then looked at the barren and burnt landscape around him.

Colleen nudged his side and brought her handkerchief to her nose. "What happened here?" she asked, trying to block the scent of the acrid air.

"Hmmm…" he mused. "Not sure. But according to this, this should be the place."

"This is horseshit!" Collen cried. "I knew we should have never trusted yer bruh-thur, Liam! Wah-di' he know about all-uhdis?"

"Hush, woman!" he admonished sternly. "Lemme think on it."

Liam bid the horses to ride around some more. Everything felt hot. The air around them—smoky and hot. And desolate. Not a soul to be seen, not an animal to be heard. Not the feel-good, lively town of New Haven Harbor his brother had written him about, but a razed heap of burnt ruin. There was nothing but heat and ash and smoke.

And human remains.

Panic rose in Colleen's voice. "We need to leave this place, Liam! I'm telling ya, the devil was here!"

"I said to hush! We should find Connor, and…"

"Find Connor?" she screamed. "There's no Connor here, milove. There's no *nobody* here! You saw all of them bodies we rode passed and…"

Liam saw something from behind one of the untouched trees and pulled back the horses again.

"Waddaya doin' now?" Colleen cried.

Liam jumped down from the carriage and walked around to investigate, hoping someone, anyone was in sight—hoping to find some inkling of life amid the devastation. "Connor?" he whispered into the thick of the trees. There was no response, but something glinted on the ground. Liam bent over to examine it. In the ash and dust and dirt, he lifted up a silver chain with a funny looking pendant on it. He held it up closer to his eyes to inspect it, and when he did, it shone with the brightness of a thousand stars. Hypnotized, he swung it back and forth and delighted in its glowing mystery. He was warm, renewed, happy… in love…

"Wah you got there, husband?" Colleen called from the carriage, but Liam was too enraptured with his treasure to hear.

The trees rustled again, and Liam walked deeper into the Black Wood. Before him stood two young children, but in the line of the setting sun, he could not tell if they were boys or girls or one of each. They bore unfamiliar shapes, like hazy smoke rising up from the ground. Was it just the smoke of the lingering fires irritating his eyes, or was he truly able to see through them? Were they even there? Was this a starved hallucination?

One of the small figures raised its arms and made a pointing gesture to the west. The other figure whispered "Lynn."

"Thank you," he smiled and stumbled out from the trees and back to the carriage.

"Liam!" Colleen screeched upon his return. "You scared the life out of me!"

"It's fine. We're going to be well. We're headed to Lynn. I know the way," he said with a faraway voice and a faraway look in his eyes.

"Huh? I don't understand. And what's that you got there?" She pointed to the silver chain spilling from his folded fingers.

"A good luck charm!" he mused.

"Give it here. Uhhh… this is wretched looking!" she complained. "Go put it back from whence it came."

"No, milove. That wretched thing just spared our lives. You will keep it."

She held it in between her fingers like a foul piece of meat. "I'll keep it, but I certainly won't wear it," she scoffed. "This is the necklace of a dead woman, Liam!"

"And now it's the necklace of a woman who was saved."

"What do you think happened here?" Colleen whispered, wide-eyed.

Liam gazed one last time into the ruin of the forest. He heard a voice cry out and children whisper quickly and softly. "A woman named Barbara set the world on fire," he said in a faraway voice.

When he broke from the trance, Liam spurred the horses and rode off to the west in search of the town of Lynn, where they eventually settled and became John and Mary Smith who had a handful of Smith children who passed on the locust-shaped pendant to their children in Ohio, and their children in Florida, and their children in Wisconsin, and their children in California.

All the way down to San Francisco,1966 to be exact.

All the way to the hands of scrawny, chain-smoking, Poppy Smith.

Chapter Eleven

Friday, June 10th 1966
Poppy's Apartment
Above The Inferno Club
San Francisco, California
Afternoon of the Waning Gibbous Moon

"**H**ow do I look?" Poppy inquired as she twirled around in front of me in the living room. She extended her long, skinny arms and spun herself on her heels. The glittery effect from her slinky dress left trails of silver before my eyes, and her short black hair whipped about her face in a blur. She looked awful. Like a hooker coming off as a wannabe model. But I couldn't tell her that because she smiled so brightly, so eagerly, that if I had said anything negative, it would have crushed her spirit into a million pieces. Her foot lost its step underneath her when she stopped spinning, and she awkwardly tripped forward. "Whoops!" she exclaimed catching her balance. And in that instant, as the fear and uncertainty of her low self-esteem washed over her face, I thought she would burst out into nervous and self-deprecating tears.

"Well, just don't do *that*!" I teased, trying to lighten the mood.

"Uuuuuhhhh!" she moaned. "Why am I so nervous, and awkward, and clutzy?" She wrung her hands together and paced across the wooden floor.

Her nervousness was catching, for I had a stake in her photoshoot as well. It was my ticket into the Black House and my shot at an audience with LaVey. I needed to do something to quell her fears, so I stood up, caught her by the shoulders, peered deeply into her eyes, and envisioned a purple hazy light swirling around us. Her face softened when the haze came into her view and she smiled at me, relaxed, and calmed down. "It's normal. You're nervous because you want this. And it's important to you. People always get the jitters when there's a lot at stake—when there's a lot to lose."

Her shoulders tensed at the word "lose" and the fear sailed across her eyes again.

"But you're not going to lose," I recovered. "You know why?"

"Why?" Her voice cracked and she tugged at the glittery fringes on the bottom of her dress.

"Because this is your destiny. This is the beginning of unlocking everything you've ever wanted."

She smiled briefly at my little pep-talk, then her face suddenly darkened. Maybe she had caught a glimpse of the truth in my eyes. I hadn't tried to hide it very well, so the storm must have been there. "You never told me how you thought I looked," she muttered.

I sighed. "You look lovely."

She scanned my face again for the truth. Her eyes darted back and forth over the circumference of my visage. "You don't mean that!" she exclaimed when the reality hit her.

"Maybe not in the context that you want it in."

"What do you mean?"

I sighed again and took a step back. "Well, I look at you now and see a girl off to a club. A girl off to have a good time. Have a few drinks, dance in a cage, maybe get fucked afterward. She's lovely. Nice to look at. Nice to have a drink with. Nice to fuck in the back alley. But, is this a girl about to start a serious career? Is this Poppy—a model about to embark on a new path? Or is this Poppy staying on the same Folsom Street bullshit?"

She gripped the fringes of the dress tighter and paused to think about what I said.

"I mean, you don't look like a girl about to go to the Church of Satan for a raw photoshoot. I don't see the real you under that heavy makeup and that spandex dress. You don't look like my Poppy."

"I don't understand," she whispered.

"Be comfortable. Be you. Walk into that photoshoot ready to go. Like you have the biggest dick in the room."

She giggled. "*You* have the biggest dick in the room!"

"Sure. I have the *only* dick in the room right now," I smirked. "But I won't be in that studio or wherever the fuck you're getting naked and shooting pictures. So, take my proverbial dick with you. Show them what's what. 'Cause when you're Poppy, and when you're *my* Poppy, that Susan Atkins ain't got nothing on you."

Her dark eyes glimmered, and she reached on her tiptoes to kiss me on the cheek. "Be right back," she said, then raced into the bathroom.

Within moments she reappeared. Changed. Different. Like she had the biggest dick in the room. She had removed the garish makeup from her face, leaving only a layer of mascara to accentuate her lashes and a pink sheen of gloss on her lips. Very muted. Very understated. Very model-like. She slicked her hair back into that popular 60s fashion cut, like that teenager over in England who was making waves in the fashion industry. *Twiggy, I think.* She had removed the ridiculous silver dress and put on a pair of tight blue jeans that flared at the bottom and an oversized white-button-down shirt that was opened down to her non-existent cleavage. And that's when I saw it—the pendant swung against her breast bones, and I knew immediately the power and gravity within it had given her a subtle boost of confidence. She twirled for me again, but this time, she was as light as air. Rejuvenated. Restored. Ready. I nodded my approval and she rushed up to kiss me hard on the mouth.

I had insisted on going with her to the shoot, and she had insisted on calling for car service. Taking the bus was beneath this future superstar, and she had wanted to make a grand entrance. Unfortunately, California Street was lined with cars on either side, and our driver dropped us off at the corner and not straight to the gates as Poppy had envisioned in her mind. She hummed and hawed with annoyance when the car sped away, and we started our trek down the city street. I threw my arm across her back and rubbed the top of her shoulder. "It's okay," I eased. "It doesn't mean anything. Everything's fine. Remember, just keep your good thoughts flowing."

I reminded myself to try to take my own advice. With the temperature still below average, it was cool enough at dusk for me to wear a light jacket—a jacket that I had tucked the *Blodheksa* book into in hopes of making my ultimate move. Because Poppy may have had a special intention for the events that evening, but I had intentions of my own.

The Black House was as advertised—a black dwelling sandwiched between two large white stucco structures. It was dwarfed between the two massive homes and didn't look much like the ominous abode Chris had made it out to be—it just looked out of place, like it didn't belong there. *Because it didn't.* It was black, yes, freshly painted so, with a peaked roof and a bow window in the front, but the neighboring homes loomed over it, and made it stick out like a sore thumb even more. A long brick staircase on the right-hand side led up to the front door with the circular window in the center of it.

"Ooooh," Poppy said quietly into my shoulder when we came upon the home at 6114 California Street. "Look at that!" She was amazed at the monstrosity of it—the glamor and mystique of it all. I wasn't so convinced.

A woman in a black velvet dress sat on the top step closest to the door smoking a cigarette. We barely noticed she was there as she seemed to blend in perfectly with the home. Her long black hair hung in her face like dyed strands of course straw. Middle-aged, she straightened out her back like a sentry on guard when we approached the steps. "Can I help you?" she said in a deep, raspy voice that startled me for a second.

Poppy broke from my side embrace and put one foot on the bottom step. The woman eyed her sharply and stood up, looming over us like a dark angel peering down from a black heaven. I felt Poppy's hesitation and uncertainty creep back into her as she took a step back and off the stair. "I... I'm one of the models for the photoshoot," she stammered, her insecurity weakening her voice.

The woman took a last drag of her cigarette and flicked the butt of it into the small walkway between the Black House and the massive white one next door. "Oh. I see."

"Susan invited me. She's the other model. Susan Atkins. She said it was okay for me to…"

"She's here," the woman interjected. "You can come on up."

Poppy looked to me with an expression of pure dread. Her eyes pleaded to me, "I need you." They begged me to follow her up the brick steps, so I moved in time with her, but the woman at the top of the landing held up her hand with her palm facing us, motioning for us to stop.

"And you?" she spat at me.

"I'm with her," I answered.

"He's my agent," Poppy said, trying to cover for me.

"He's your boyfriend, doll face," the woman corrected. "No boyfriends allowed."

I pushed the small of Poppy's back, urging her to continue up the stairs. "Knock 'em dead," I whispered with a quick kiss to her shoulder, "I'll wait for you right here." With a deep inhale, she tussled her hair back, gulped down the last of her anxiety, and glided up to the landing. The woman opened the black wooden door, and Poppy crept herself inside, swallowed by the darkness of the mysterious interior.

As the door shut with a thud, the woman turned her attention back to me and descended the stairs. "So, Boyfriend. You just gonna stand here and wait for your girl?"

I nodded. "Yep. Seems that way. But I'd much rather go inside and get a feel for what's going on."

"Worried about what they're doing in there?" she said with a hint of smarminess.

"No. I couldn't care less about all that. I want to see LaVey. I would like to talk to him about some things."

She laughed a forced but hearty laugh in my face. Her smoky breath filled my nostrils. "The Doctor doesn't see just anyone, ya know."

"Oh, I know. Chris told me…"

"Chris?" she questioned. "Big Chris with the red sideburns, or Little Chris with the greasy hair?"

"Um…" I stammered. "Greasy hair, I guess."

"Oh, Chris S. He's trying to recruit. Nice boy. Drinks too much but nice boy."

"Yes. He said he would arrange a meeting for me with Anton."

"Dr. LaVey," the woman corrected.

"Yes, of course. Dr. LaVey."

She turned her face to the side and narrowed her eyebrows. "Why would Dr. LaVey see you, though? You're not a church member. How do you know Chris?" Her blue eyes looked gold against the setting sunlight, and by her general demeanor, I knew it would take some fancy talking to plead my case.

I waved my hand in front of me, creating a shimmer of energy between us. Her eyes flashed like most people's do when they see what they think they didn't see, or think they see something that's there, or isn't. Is their mind playing tricks on them, or are there really stars dropped down from heaven in front of their eyes? It's the look of wonder when it marries pure confusion. It's the look of the weak-minded under the simplest of spells. It's the look of the want and the need to *know*. Her eyes followed the trail of my hand, and her gaze broke when I shoved them into my jeans pocket. "We met at the Crescent City Café over on Folsom," I explained. "I research occult studies, and we got to talking about the organization."

"You're a student of the cause?"

"More like a trailblazer. I have a text that I think Dr. LaVey would be very interested in seeing. After all, he's studied the paranormal in the past. I think what I have would be of great interest to not just him, but to the future of the church."

Because if LaVey is who he says he is, if LaVey wields the power he claims to wield, and if LaVey truly has a connection to the old ones, he will be able to see the text and together we will find the Blodheksa and crack open the world.

I sent my inner thought to the woman's mind, and she paused, listening to them, letting the words and music of it flood her head and wash down into her chest. She shivered. Her whole body did a rigid shake and she said, "Oh, someone must have walked over my grave," but I don't think she realized the words had come out of her mouth.

Someone, somewhere, I said back into her head, and she snapped out of her semi-trance and looked at me like she had just woken up from a quick nap.

She placed one hand on a hip and pushed her hair from her face with the other. "You know Chris is a nobody, though. He's just a spectator."

As I had suspected.

But Chris has a gift.

She sighed. "Fine, well, if you want to leave this *sacred text* with me, I can see that Dr. LaVey gets it…"

"No. It's best if I…"

"Listen, I've been with the organization since before it was called the Order of the Trapezoid. I've been a loyal disciple of our Black Pope. I'm a trusted member of…"

"No," I said again. "I wish I could, but it's important for me to be there when he sees it."

Cause I'm not about to leave an ancient text in the hands of some pretender…

"Then let me see it first."

My heart doesn't normally sink, but for a second right then, it did. Because I knew that no matter what I said or did, or whatever glamouring I conjured, she would not be able to see the writings within the book. She might not be able to see the book at all. The cloaking magic embedded by Aizel centuries ago still held strong.

But I had no other choice. So, I mustered up my strongest and best glamouring and pulled the book from my inner jacket pocket.

The woman took it gingerly with both hands, and I knew she could hear the shadowy voices from within it. Her eyes widened as she cradled it in her palms, but when her fingers danced across the cover to open the pages, it revealed all but an empty book. Her once look of wonder quickly turned to derision as the music of it all ceased and was overtaken by her hideous laughter. She was false. I knew she was false, but something inside me had hoped she wasn't—had hoped that she would be able to feel or sense something or even see something without my intervention. And like I had feared, if LaVey had false disciples in his midst, then most likely he wouldn't be able to see or feel or hear the *Blodheksa* book without my help either.

She closed the book shut and returned it to me. "I'm sorry, but I think you're tripping on some wild shit, Boyfriend."

I took a step back and put the book into my jacket pocket. It rested closely and gently to my chest. Once again, I surveyed the Black House, but this time with my Aevir eyes and senses, and only then could I truly see—a dark well of nothing. No layers to be peeled away, no real magic to be had. Just some parlor tricks and empty souled people milling around behind the walls of blackness. Some of them had "X's" on their heads, but for the most part, it was all a game devoid of the capability to accomplish my goal. There was no New Eden to be had here.

Dejected, I hung my head low, and before I could open my mouth to respond to her, the front door flung open, and Poppy appeared in the threshold. Tears streamed down her face, and her shirt was disheveled and untucked. She bent over as she quickly hopped down the staircase and hobbled to put on her platform sandals.

"Poppy!" I exclaimed at the unanticipated sight.

"Let's go, Trent!" she screamed as she stumbled passed the woman.

"What happened? Are you okay?"

"He… he kicked me out!" she screamed as she grabbed onto my elbow and marched furiously away from the house and practically ran down the block.

"Who? Who kicked you out?" I asked when I caught up to her. "Tell me what happened."

"The photographer! Leif Something-or-other. I don't know what happened. Susan took off her clothes. He started taking pictures of her. It was all sexy and stuff. And then I was up. I took off my shirt, and he started babbling in another language. Some weird shit. He called me a… a… a *heksa*? Then he said to leave, and Susan would just do the rest of the shoot without me. What the fuck does that even mean? Heksa? Fucking for-eigner! Fucking asshole!"

"It's okay," I said calmly. "You said the photographer's name is Leif?"

"Yeah. Leif. Leif Something. Hail-something? Heil-something? I don't remember. But I swear, he fucked up my shit, and I need him to die!"

"Stop!" I admonished. "You know how these crazy Hollywood types are. Who knows why he didn't want to pho-tograph you!"

But I knew. With a name like Leif, it could only mean one thing—he was from the old country and knew of the old ways. And I was willing to bet anything that the second he saw Poppy's pendant, he wanted nothing to do with her. Of course, he misnamed her as a witch because a witch Poppy was not. But when one wears the true symbols and tools of one, it's hard not to…

"You have to do something, Trent!" she begged, pounding her fists frantically on my chest. "Please! I know you know things. I've seen you do things! Make this right for me! Do some of your magic shit!"

"Alright, alright," I said. "Lower your voice. Let's not get out of control. Let's go get something to eat and we'll talk about all that later. No need to get bent out of shape now."

She swiped both of the backs of her hands across her eyes and down her cheeks, wiping the tears from her face. Her breaths were slowing down to a calmer pace. "Okay, okay," she breathed. "But you will help me, right?"

"Sure, Hellflower. I'll help you. Let's just go somewhere to cool off. I think we both were disappointed today."

Chapter Twelve

Saturday, June 18th 1966
The Crescent City Café
San Francisco, California
Night of the New Moon

Pina waddled over with my cup of black coffee and set it down in front of me. "Here ya go, hon," she said with a smile. She took out a silver flask from underneath her work apron and gave my mug a shot of Kahlua, then put her finger to her closed lips and hissed, "Shhhh." I winked at her and raised my cup as a sort of salute. She pat me on the shoulder and drifted to the next table. Pina was good people. I actually enjoyed my time working for her, which was surprising enough. I wasn't the type for small talk or menial labor. My talents were more suited to more grandiose lines of work, so being a handyman was somewhat beneath me. But in the grand scheme of things, I had done worse than this in my lifetimes, so when I thought about it, I was grateful for the opportunity to lie low for the time being.

The string of performers that night had been god-awful—some of the worst to step foot inside the café. Pina knew it, too. I watched her face screw up in agony when an ex-beatnik banged on her drum and sang a song she had titled "War." War it was, for the assault of the awful cacophony on the

crowd's ears was torturous. And the poetry readings of the evening weren't anything to write home about either! I think Pina was slipping alcohol into everyone's drinks just to keep them happy and numb to the constant onslaught of trash.

Suddenly, Chris rose from one of the tables up front and made his way to the stage. I didn't even know he was in the café—hadn't even sensed his presence. That fact alone gave me reason to pause, so I put down my spiked drink for I didn't want any more influence from the beverage to cloud me, and I paid close attention to Chris and his movements.

Sometimes when the moon is darkest, the light inside takes over and illuminates what can't normally be seen. I remembered one of my sister's teachings from a long time ago. Her voice was crisp and clear, like she was standing right next to me in the now, and not six thousand miles away twelve hundred years ago. And yes, the new moon had darkened the sky with the absence of its light, so I tucked Blodwyn's words into my chest and let the remnants of the old power quicken and sputter and spark inside me. I blinked a few times to re-shift my focus— to draw the energy from the center of myself and tune in my vision to break through the veil of reality.

Something like a growl rumbled in my head putting me on high alert. There was a marked change in Chris's appearance and demeanor as he glided up the steps to the stage. The air surrounding him was dense—thick and cloudy. Something manifested in a circle around his feet like tendrils of roots jutting up from the ground trying to form themselves into a tree. Shadowy branches crept up behind his head and bobbed up and down in the breeze-filled forest, and the features of his face melted together and swirled around like ice cream being squeezed into a sugar cone from an industrial machine. I was taken aback, startled at first. I hadn't seen him in about a week, and this growth of energy, of power, of *something* inside him was developing at a rapid pace. I still didn't know if he was cognizant of it yet, but judging from the images of my preternatural eyes, if he *didn't* know, he would soon.

He tapped the mic three times and cleared his throat. The sound boomed off the café walls and seemed to bring everyone to attention. "In Nomine Dei Nostri Satanas, Luciferi Excelsi.

In the Name of Satan, Ruler of the Earth, I invite the Forces of Hell to bestow their great power upon us this year, 1966, the year of our Lord, year one. Anno Satanas."

Someone in the crowd echoed back, "Anno Satanas!"

Another person raised their hand in the air and shouted, "Hail Satan."

Curious, I thought, *this church thing might actually be catching on.*

"Into the Black," he began, and this time I realized he wasn't reading from a piece of paper. This time he had the poem memorized. *Just like a good preacher would...* "When we step into the Black. When we give ourselves over to the Night—the Knight of the Night. When we live and die by the words of the prophet, only then can our souls be cleansed. We are we. The light and the black know no bounds. It is blurred. We are blurred. We are singular, yet we are Legion. *We* are Satan. To thine own self, be true. The Black is within us all." The words circled around the throng, and I saw each one dangle in the air, dripping with blood. Unbeknownst to the crowd, and to Chris himself, the words pierced the skin of every person in the room. They needled their way under the top layers of flesh and spread throughout their bodies like an invisible, gangrenous infection. Whether they knew it or not, the words made the people stop, and pause, and think, and question the nature of their own realities—even if for a second.

This unchecked power worried me—filled me with a flash of dread. For the first time in a long time, I was legitimately concerned about the existence of another, and suddenly a new voice came bounding into my memory, pulling back the curtain and guiding me to what I ultimately had to do. Aizel's voice...

There are others who would try to subvert our power for their own gain. Don't assume that we are all on the same side. Others are jealous of our strength and seek to take it as their own. There are those who would love nothing more than to see us fail in our goal to cleanse this world. They would love nothing more than to sabotage our bloodline's mission and seek to destroy the hope of the new world we wish to create. Just because two beings walk amongst the dark doesn't mean they are kin.

The crowd sent up a round of applause. The two followers who had parroted back Chris's words stood up and cheered, and I remained in my seat. My eyes were trained hard on him, and he finally felt them boring holes in his side. He looked over, and I waved him on to join me.

"What's up, man?" he said when he trotted over.

"Nothing. Just hanging," I replied nonchalantly. "Figured you'd be over at Inferno with your girl."

"Susan?" he crowed. "Nah. She's not my girl. And she's gone, anyway. Haven't seen or heard from her in days. But I knew she was like that. Trouble."

"Listen man, I was over at the Black House the other night and…"

"Yeah, yeah," he cut me off, "I heard about that. You name dropping me and shit. Trying to get me in trouble or something?" he smirked.

I chuckled with him but was raging on the inside. "No. Nothing like that. I just didn't trust that woman at the door. I have a book on occult studies—like I told you, it's something I've been working on for years. I think it's of prime interest to the church, and when that woman wanted to take it from me, I just couldn't let her. I need assurances that it'll get into LaVey's hands."

Chris snorted with derision. "Laura told me all about that book."

My skin crawled at his cockiness, solidifying that yes, he was changing. He was evolving. He was growing into something he couldn't control.

And I had to stop him.

"Oh, yeah," I said, playing dumb. "What did she say about it?"

"Nothing, man. Nothing."

"Seriously," I probed. "What's the deal? You wanna see it, too?"

He waved his hand dismissively in the air. "Well, you know what they say: the road to hell is paved with good intentions."

"Look, I totally understand your reluctance to get me in to see LaVey. Totally. Why don't you come with me, get the book, get it to him, and we'll take it from there. I promise, there's a lot I have to offer in terms of the church. I've been all around the world. I've *seen* shit, man." On the word "seen" I sent out a blast to his mind with the force of a stun-gun. It paralyzed him momentarily and put him into a quasi-stupor. I stood up and gestured with my thumb to the back door that led to the staircase connecting my apartment to the café. Quickly, he rose and followed me.

Upstairs, I directed Chris to take a seat at the small, circular table in the kitchenette area. I put up one finger to indicate I'd be right back, slipped away into my bedroom, procured the book, and dropped it on the table in front of him. His face lit up when it came into his sight, and he pushed his hair back from his face so as to see it better and in full view.

"This," I said, rapping my forefinger on the leather cover, "this is my life's work, so to speak. My life's mission."

Entranced, his eyes glazed over with a faraway look, and that creeping sense of dread worked its way back into my chest. "Can I?" he asked, motioning his chin to the book.

I nodded, and he picked it up. A surge of heat radiated in the room when his fingers made contact with the aged binding. Again, I put myself on high alert.

He ran his hand over the cover and closed his eyes. "Blodheksa," he whispered like a man whispering a dirty secret into his lover's ear. His swoon disturbed me. Sickened me. Filled me with a murderous rage.

"You can see that?" I asked.

He ignored me and opened the book, turning the pages slowly, methodically. He inhaled the scent of the book—the sweet smell of power, the ancient aroma of decay. He breathed it in through his nose and savored it all, and I wondered if he was able to feel the vibrations of it and hear its songs.

"Yeah," he mused. "It's so… *loud.*"

In that moment, I knew Chris wasn't there. He wasn't in my apartment. He was off in the woods with the ancient ones, singing along with the gods of the night, learning the mysteries of the runes in the forests, dancing naked under the silver trees. But more importantly, he was learning how to open the gates and bring on the New Eden. As he absorbed the power of the book, his eyes fluttered into the back of his head, and a translucent dome of energy formed around him. A funny sensation gripped me from the pit of my stomach. It tingled at first, then gathered up to my esophagus making me feel like I was going to vomit. And I realized Chris was pulling me, my energy, into him.

There are others who would try to subvert our power for their own gain. Aizel's words replayed in my head, and I panicked.

I grabbed a kitchen knife from the countertop and slid up behind Chris at the table. I leaned over and pushed the book away from him. Broken from his trance, he tilted his head to the side to bring me into his sight. "Huh?" he said dreamily.

With one hand I gripped the back of his head, and with the other, I ran the blade of the knife across his neck. Chris's blood hissed and sprayed over the table, the droplets coated the pages of where he had been reading, and he gurgled and choked and thrashed about in the chair. With all my force, I tried to hold him in place, tried to keep him still so his blood would drain out in a glorious fountain, but he was wild and fierce and hard to contain. There was no other choice but to slice him deeper. I pulled his head back harder, widening the gap at his throat, and again, ran the knife across. He looked up at me with wide, desperate eyes, like an animal brought to the inevitable slaughter. I must have severed something deep because the gurgling stopped, and his neck wobbled effortlessly against my grasp. Once the gush of his blood sputtered to a puttering spray, I dipped his head forward like closing a dainty music box and rested his lifeless body hunched on the table.

The road to hell is paved with good intentions. I heard Chris's voice say.

No. No, it's not. It's drenched in blood, I thought. *The sacrificial blood for the new moon.*

Suffice it to say, I felt better. My vision became clearer. I was renewed and regenerated as I absorbed what I could of Chris's life force. No longer did the draining feeling vex me. No longer did I have the impending feeling of doom. No longer did I have a true adversary to rival my abilities and subvert my mission. *For now...*

I also knew that my time in San Francisco had come to an unceremonious end, so I showered and changed, packed up my pertinent belongings, cleaned up what I could (because I really did like Pina, and felt a little guilty about the mess), and left. There was one more loose end to tie up—Poppy was getting ready for her shift at the Inferno, so I made my way over to her apartment before she went downstairs.

"What are you doing here?" she questioned when she threw open the door.

Just as I had suspected, she was dressed in her go-go outfit ready to dance in the cage. Her hair was slicked to the side, and her dark makeup was caked onto her face.

"Listen, there's no time," I said breathlessly, pushing my way passed her and into the apartment.

"Trent! I have to get to work! I'm already late for..."

"No! You're not going to work downstairs. You're going back to California Street. The Black House."

She narrowed her eyes and bounced on her hip. "What the fuck are you talking about?"

"There's no time to explain, but I fixed it. I fixed everything for you."

Her face brightened up with curiosity. "What do you mean?"

I grabbed her by the elbow and led her to her bedroom. "It's a long story, no time to get into detail," I said with mock urgency in my voice. "I spoke to Chris, and he got the details. He got me in to speak with the people at the Black House. Turns out that photographer is from the old country, and your necklace," I pointed to the pendant dangling around her neck, "reminded him of some ancient witchcraft stuff, and he freaked out. Said he didn't want any bad luck surrounding the shoot."

"That doesn't make sense. He was taking pictures for the Church of Satan!"

I shrugged my shoulders. "I dunno. Whaddoo I know? This is what they told me."

"It's late Trent! Why would he agree to a photoshoot this late?"

"He's leaving town tomorrow. *They* said *he* said it's now or never. Something about Susan's pictures not coming out the way he wanted and..."

Poppy jumped up and down in place and flailed her arms wildly in the air. "Are you serious? Are you really, really serious?" A smile like an upside-down rainbow plastered on her face exposing every single one of the nubby teeth in her mouth.

"Yes! I'm serious! But you have to go now! Like now, *now*! Change, scrub off that makeup, make like you were last week!"

She squealed in delight and bounced around the room nearly tripping over her clothing as she disrobed. "You did it! You did your magic, didn't you?" she called over the running water from the bathroom sink.

"Oh, I did something, alright," I mumbled in spite of myself.

"Trent! Should I call a cab? Or take the bus? Maybe I should walk over there."

"No, no, no. Hop in a cab. It's quickest. But you gotta hurry, Poppy. You're gonna miss it!"

"Okay, okay!" she sang as she stumbled out of the bathroom. She had put on the same outfit she had worn the day of the actual photoshoot, styled her hair the same, and even mimicked the same makeup palette. "Thumbs up?" she asked.

"Uh uh," I said wagging a finger in front of her face.

She frowned, defeated.

I put my opened palm in front of her. "The necklace. Give it here. That's what got you in this mess in the first place."

She open-palm smacked her forehead. "Stupid, me!" she exclaimed, looped it from around her neck, and dropped it into my hand.

A shock of electricity pulsed up my arm, and I breathed in heavily. I was calm. Whole. With the book and the necklace both in my possession, and the surge of Chris's new power flowing through me, I felt like I could do anything! I was on top of the world! I could punch a hole *through* the world! "Don't worry, Hellflower, I'll guard it for you. Keep it safe until you get back. I'll wait for you here."

Poppy bounced up to me with pure happiness and excitement. She pulled my head in close to hers and kissed me deeply on the mouth. "You better be ready for me when I get back," she cooed. "I owe you more than you know."

I kissed her back—slowly, seductively, sending her images of all the naughty things I was going to do to her upon her arrival. Then I pulled away and stopped the flow of images. "Never mind that now. Just keep your good thoughts flowing."

"And you keep your actions to match. Be a good boy while I'm away, 'cause when I come home, I'm gonna need you to be very, very bad." She kissed me one last time and trotted out the door.

I waited. I don't know for how long, but I played the entire scene out in my mind's eye: Poppy flagging down a cab, getting in, saying in her sweet voice "California Street, please," the driver pulling away. I waited and watched how it unfolded in my head—how she would saunter up to the Black House, maybe be met by Laura or one of the other church disciples, explain who she was and what she was doing there maybe three or four times before the reality of it sank in—the reality that I had lied to her and there was no photoshoot.

When the time was right, I left the apartment and grabbed the bag I had hidden in the hallway. I flagged a cab of my own.

"San Francisco International Airport," I instructed the driver. "Departures."

Part 3

Chapter Thirteen

Monday, April 18th 1977
Badlands Bar
Minot, North Dakota
Night of the New Moon

The pool stick made forceful contact with the old white cue ball. It streaked across the ratty green velvet of the tabletop and crashed into the perfect triangle on the opposite side. The crack of the balls filled the room and a few people at the bar swiveled their heads around to see if any would find their way to one of the side holes. Multiple did. I jabbed my pool stick into the floor and chuckled.

"Son of a bitch!" my opponent exclaimed. "Alright, call it again."

"Stripes, of course."

"Yeah, yeah," he rolled his eyes. "It's always stripes. Go on, take your turn. I'll go get the beers."

"Yeah, you do that," I called over, lining up my next shot.

Downtown Minot was a busy place if you could call North Dakota *busy*. Landlocked at all sides, south of Canada, middle of practically nowhere—it was the perfect place for someone like me to disappear to. After I had left the mess of San Francisco behind, I had traveled around for a few years until I stumbled across this little town. It was the type of place

where everyone knew each other, but a person was afforded the luxury to be whoever they wanted. What was most attractive about Minot was that it was considered a trucking town as it was perfectly situated on interstates 2 and 52 for west and east and 83 for north and south. The locals referred to them as easy access points. So, with the Air Force Base in town and truckers coming in and out from all directions, there was always a rotation of people, faces, and stories, and I blended in very well. Blended in, and laid low: Trent Forest—thirty years old, handyman extraordinaire, recently divorced, ex-wife wiped him clean, looking for a new start kind of guy—and voila, instant life. I made this look too easy.

The Badlands Bar was a few blocks from where I lived downtown. It was the general hangout for the local menfolk to grab a beer after work, or just get away from the wife and kids for a few hours. The truckers liked it because they knew they could pull on in, grab a beer, shoot some pool, and head on out with no hassle. There was no having to put on airs to impress someone, no bar floozy hanging over your shoulder looking for an expensive good time, no having to make meaningless chitchat in the hopes that someone *might* go home with you or give you head in the backseat of your car. It was a true "man's place"—not many women frequented there, which was nice. It was a relief. After my last experience with a woman, I had sworn off the female form for a while, so I enjoyed the relaxing atmosphere.

My opponent came back with the beers and rested them on the edge of the pool table. "You go?" he asked.

"No, no. I waited for you. Only fair for you to be present when I kick your ass again, especially since you'll have to buy the next round when I win… *again*."

He rolled his eyes, "You're killing me, Forest! I call bullshit. You have an unfair advantage. You fucking get all the practice you need while I'm pulling all-nighters out there on the road. I think I should get some kind of advantage."

"Aw, baloney!" I retorted. "Stop being a punk and play some real pool!"

He squared up his pool stick and came at me as if to stab me in the stomach. I lurched back with a "hey now!" and laughed.

"Come on," he said with defeat. "Let's get the torture over with."

And with that, I sent the cue ball sailing across the table, hitting my mark, and cracking some more striped balls into their pockets. Silas chugged his beer and hung his head down low with playful shame. It was over rather quickly.

I met Silas a few months back. He was a trucker who drove for just about any company that would hire him on the pretense that the route he would have to travel was from New York to North Dakota or vice versa. Apparently, it was the only itinerary he liked to drive or felt comfortable with, so his work was never steady. I had asked him about it once, and he said something about his family and having a place in both New York and North Dakota and that he didn't really need the money because of some inheritance he got when he was twenty and that he only did it because he enjoyed traveling. But I saw right through it. It was the fountain of lies that flowed from his lips, much like my own. Because in Minot, North Dakota, anyone could be whoever they wanted to be, and I chose to be Trent Forest, and this clean-cut looking trucker chose to be thirty-two-year-old Silas Creed. He was tall and unassuming in stature, and for his line of work, he kept himself neat and clean-cut. At first glance, one could have easily pegged him for a military guy, but his pockmarked face and icy blue eyes gave him an air of danger and mystery.

We would make small talk when he would pass through town every few weeks or so, have a few beers at the bar, shoot some pool. Some other guys would come in and out occasionally, but it was usually different faces each weekend. Except for me. Except for Silas. And even though I knew he was a straight up liar, there was something about him that drew me in, not in a sexual way or anything like that, but hanging out with him got me thinking... in all my years walking on this planet, never have I ever had a friendship with another man. I was raised by women, had friendships with women, had relationships with women, everything was always female-centric. Was this the first time I could say I had a male friend?

But was he? Was he really? Because I knew by all means and standards true friends didn't usually lie about the most basic of things, and we were both enjoying each other's company under false pretenses. Did he know I was lying to him, too? Maybe this was how things were with men. I didn't know. This was new territory for me, but there was something about Silas that attracted me to him—*attract* as in *pulled, drew me in,* caught my attention, put my senses on mid-alert. There was something familiar about him. Something off, but not quite so. I couldn't put my finger on it. To be honest, I hadn't tried.

After the last of the balls fell noisily into the cup, I tilted my head up and glared at him through the shaggy hair that fell forward into my face. "Another?" I asked.

He took the last swig from his bottle and waved his arm in the air. "Nah, man. I'm good. Done for the night."

"Fair enough," I said.

I walked over and sat at the bar. He followed, waved two fingers at the bartender and lit a cigarette. He slid the pack and his silver Zippo across to me, and I pushed it back, refusing the offer. "Oh yeah, right. I forgot. You don't smoke. Why don't you smoke, Trent? You drink, that is for sure."

I shrugged. "Never really liked it."

"What are you, a fucking woman?" he laughed.

"Fuck you, Silas. You'll see, when that cancer eats your insides out…"

"Cancer shmancer!" he huffed dismissively and blew a plume of smoke into the air in front of him. "We're all gonna die sometime, right?"

Some of us… I thought.

He glanced at me from the corner of his eye—a gesture so subtle that a normal person wouldn't have noticed, but for me, it sent a shiver up my spine to the base of my skull and rang a low-sounding humming alarm into my ears. For a second, I wondered if he had heard my inside thought, but quickly threw that thought out of my mind. It was impossible. He had never given me any sign that…

"So," he began, grinding the butt of his cigarette into the ashtray at the bar, but he was interrupted by the dinging of the bell in the threshold of the front door.

Three men entered the bar—hard-looking lumberjack types with long hair and flannel shirts and tan work boots.

Just another bunch of truckers, I thought, but when they spotted Silas at the bar, their eyes went wide, and they approached us.

"Silas fucking Creed!" the burly one boomed.

Silas spun around in the barstool. "Holy shit, dude! You guys made it!"

The men gathered around each other with beefy, one-armed man hugs and hearty back-pats, and "heys" and "whoahs" and "what's happenings?" I sank back in my seat a little, obviously the odd-one-out in this reunion. They all spoke fervently at once and on top of each other, but I managed to zone in on their voices and isolate the different flow of the conversations.

They had just flown in from New York.

The plane ride was awful. Craig got sick.

They were staying a few days, picking up a job in Roosevelt Heights, and heading back to New York.

The last job had been successful. They all seemed to be happy about that.

"Oh guys!" Silas said, clapping my upper arm, "This is Trent. Trent, this is Craig, John, and Phil. Buddies of mine from the Big Apple."

I wanted to say I figured that out already, but I opted for a head nod and a "hey."

They eyed me coolly, and with a sense of hesitation that sent the alarm bells ringing in my head once again. My lack of understanding male-to-male interactions was getting the best of me, and an uncomfortable feeling worked its way deep inside my stomach like something gnawing at my gut, telling me to be cautious, cautious, ever so cautious.

"Where you staying?" Silas asked them.

"Where else would we stay?" the red-head named Phil bellowed.

A grin slithered on Silas's face. "Exactly what I wanted to hear! Let's go." He rose from the barstool and looked back to me. "Hey, Trent. Why don't you come hang with us for a while?"

I hesitated, remembering the weird glares the others had given me before. "Nah, man. Thanks. I'm cool. I got a job early in the morning. I should head home."

"Fuck that!" Silas exclaimed. "Cancel it. Come party with us!"

I looked up from my drink, and something like a red "X" danced across Silas's face. The bells in my head got louder. A wave of weightlessness invaded the pit of my stomach, as my curiosity took root in my spine. "Fine," I said, "I'm in."

Loud barking pierced through the crisp night as Phil's rented Thunderbird slid up along the rocky side-road. The property was mid-sized with a fenced in yard, with a one-story house situated perfectly in the middle of it all. We were off the main drag, down side street after side street, to this nestled hide-away Silas called home. It was small and cottage-like—the perfect bachelor pad for someone to live in part-time. In the darkness, a shadowy figure raced on all fours back and forth behind the chain-link fence—a large looming creature who looked like a werewolf when it stood up on its hind legs and growled at us as we emptied out of the vehicle. "Let me go get her. She gets a little skittish around strangers," Silas said and went around the side of the house. Inside, Craig and Phil plopped down on the orange plush sofa in the living room, while John went to the kitchen to get more beer. I stood uncomfortably in the hallway that separated the two rooms, watching the strangers intently, assessing the situation.

Suddenly the backdoor at the end of the hallway opened and the beast sauntered in tethered to a long leather leash. Black hair and long snout, it stared me down with wild eyes and growled against its bared teeth—teeth that would easily and happily tear me to shreds if given the chance. *Or the command.* This was no ordinary German Shepherd, either—straight from the bowels of hell, I wondered where its other two heads were. Something dark and archaic resided in the animal, an energy that I had instantly sensed with my own animal instincts. The beast was massive and had wasted no time letting me know I had invaded its territory.

Silas appeared behind it and closed the storm door. He looked at me with a curious expression—his eyes wondered if he should let the dog go and attack me or reign the beast in and heel to obedience.

But I remained perfectly still, unfazed by animal's warning, and locked eyes with it. *With her.* "Easy, girl," I said in my mind to her, but she continued to snarl and buck against the leash as if to lunge at me.

I relaxed my shoulders and slouched forward a little, as if I were bowing in awe of her enormous presence. There was no denying this beautiful being with her thick coat of jet-black fur and unusual set of pale blue eyes. Even from the distance of the hallway, they pierced through me and spoke to my inner core. She settled down a little and her aggressive snarls gave way to a low rumble growl. I absorbed the rhythm and cadence of it into a hollow in my chest where I transformed it back into a song—an ancient song reserved only for witches and their familiars.

"Oh shit!" one of the guys called out. "Looks like Trent's met Genesis!"

"Don't worry, dude! Genny will only take one of your balls!"

They all laughed, but I ignored them and continued my stare down with the creature as I continued to hum the song to her, trying to lull it into submission. And as we watched each other, her eyes flashed from blue to gray to brown to black, and I knew she was ready to receive my spell. "Peace," I said directly into her mind. "Peace, sweet Genesis," and I waved my hand in the air. A trail of stars only it could see manifested in the space between us and calmed it instantly.

Genesis gave one last hard tug against the leash. Silas was taken off guard and had fumbled with his grip. The dog came bounding down the hallway, and I bent down at my knees to receive its playful kisses to my face.

"What the fuck?" one of the guys in the other room exclaimed.

Genesis licked my face furiously, and I pet and scratched at her ears and neck like we were old friends. Silas stood frozen by the door for a moment with a look on his face that I couldn't place. Amazement? Disgust? Fear? Jealousy? It was hard to tell.

"Wow," he finally said with some sarcasm attached. "Looks like Genesis likes you! Genny hates everyone she meets the first time."

"Ain't that the truth," John bellowed. "I still have the scar on my hand!"

"What can I say, I'm good with animals," I retorted, but Silas ignored me, made his way to the living room and sat on the floor in front of the couch.

I continued to pet her and nuzzled my face into the crook of her neck. "Hey Silas," I called over, "she's not a full Shepherd, is she."

"Wolfdog," he replied. "Half wolf, half Shepherd."

"Makes sense," I whispered into her ear and stood back up. Genny's tail wagged frantically, and she rubbed up against my knee looking for more attention. I couldn't help but smile at my new regal friend.

"Everything good," Silas finally said to no one in particular.

John mumbled an "Uh huh."

"Everyone okay?" he asked again.

"Five by five," Phil answered. "I mean, other than the fact that it clearly wasn't her…"

"Again," Craig grumbled.

Silas nodded confidently and scratched the black layer of stubble on his scarred chin. "Craig, you were on clean up, right? No problems with that?"

"Nope, none at all," he answered.

"And our man from New York? How's he holding up with everything?"

"Like a good little soldier," John beamed. "He's doing just fine."

The vibe in the room shifted, and my preternatural senses picked up on something else beneath the surface—something beyond my own lingering power in the house. I quickly sensed they weren't just talking about work, or trucking, or a job they all participated in.

"You guys are old friends," I said, feigning innocent curiosity.

"Something like that," John laughed.

"Whereabouts in New York?" I pried, digging for some more info on the four. "I'm pretty familiar with Long Island. Have some people out that way."

"Untermyer Park, in Yonkers," Phil answered, and Craig slapped his knee hard.

Silas raised his hand and shook his head as if to say, "stop, it's ok," and the three others clammed up and went silent.

"Oh, cool," I responded like an idiot because I was too focused on their subtle exchanges.

"It'll probably be on the news by now," Craig said, and John walked over and turned on the small television. It hummed and sprang to life with static, and he rotated the antennae to make the picture come into focus.

I moved into the living room with Genny wagging her tail right behind me. I sat next to Silas with our backs against the coffee table in front of the sofa and again, he gave me that sideways look from the bar before. "What are we watching?" I quietly asked him, but he didn't respond.

Not verbally at least.

History is about to be made, I heard a gravelly voice say.

Phil cracked open a can of beer and shouted, "History is about to be made, gentlemen!"

Silas and I looked at each other with a knowing glance. And a drumbeat sounded in the distance. And Genesis wiggled her massive body in between us. And trees swayed in the forest. And a song was being sung in the tear in the sky. And Silas's eyes changed from brown, to green, to gold, to gray, and then they were *my* eyes set inside his chiseled face with his crewcut hair. Genny turned his face back and forth from Silas to me in confusion. Her dog senses picked up on the thickness in the air that grew in between us and the swapping glamour of our faces. I was Silas, Silas was me. And poor Genny, too confused and upset, squealed and ran off into one of the back rooms of the house.

The room buzzed when the news program popped onto the screen and the newscaster announced, "Breaking news out of The Bronx, New York."

Craig, John, and Phil applauded and cheered like teenagers at a rock concert.

Just watch, the voice said again to me.

You've got my attention now, I responded in my mind, and Silas smirked.

Chapter Fourteen

Monday, April 18th 1977
Silas's House
Minot, North Dakota
Night of the New Moon

C raig shushed everyone in the room and leaned forward to turn up the volume knob on the television. The female news anchor wore heavy makeup—blue eyeshadow and red blush—and her soft blonde hair fell in layered wisps that framed her face. I couldn't help but think she looked like that blonde actress from the TV show "Charlie's Angels." Farrah Something-or-other. Only this one was Candy Dobson, and her expressionless face and non-affect vocal tone left much to be desired. An Angel, she certainly was not.

"Here we go, boys!" John announced, and Craig hushed him again.

"The .44 Caliber Killer has struck again," Candy continued. Her eyes widened with terror, but it was plain to see she was desperately fighting against her natural inclination to show emotion. As part of her job, she needed to be cool, calm, collected, and most of all, unbiased, but it was obvious that reporting this story was getting the best of her. The picture on the screen was blurry and small, and I wished I could have seen what color her eyes were. Wished I could have swept into

them and implanted all kinds of villainous thoughts inside her pea-brain. *That would have been amusing.*

"The .44 Caliber Killer?" I said quietly to Silas.

"Yeah, I hate that fucking name," he grumbled.

"Just wait! Just wait! She's gotta say it! She's gotta!" Phil crowed.

"Mister fucking 44!" Craig chimed.

Candy looked away from the teleprompter for a half of a second, probably to suck in some air and regain her composure for the camera. *"Shortly after 3:00 AM, 18-year-old Valentina Suriani and her boyfriend, 20-year-old Alexander Esau were attacked while they were parked in Esau's car about a block from Suriani's Bronx home. Suriani was seated behind the steering wheel when three shots from a .44 caliber revolver came through a closed window. A resident nearby called the shots in to the police. Suriani was killed instantly. Esau died hours later at Jacobi Hospital..."*

"Okay, okay, now we're talking," John said smoothly.

"...this is the fourth similar attack with the same weapon in the last eight months, police experts say."

I furrowed my brow in concern. "Wait. Fourth?"

Phil shot to the edge of the couch and got up in my face. "Oh, c'mon man!" he spat with aggravation. "Tell me this isn't the first time you're hearing about these killings! It's only been going on since..."

"Would you shut the fuck up and listen to the TV?" Silas commanded, keeping his focus on the program.

Phil's mouth closed with a *pop*, and he sat back, and I watched Silas's face brighten as Candy doled out more information about the slayings. The light from the TV reflected in his wide eyes and he delighted in the details like a child in a toy store being allowed to choose whatever item he wanted. It made him salivate, as a swirl of darkness rose from the floor and engulfed the both of us in a magnetic dome. While its pressure felt heavy on my chest, it gave me the feeling of weightlessness, as if I were levitating off the ground with Silas next to me. The others were unaffected. They hooted and hollered, untouched by the shift in the air, but Genny felt it, and she howled in the back room—long, low, and deep.

"...yesterday's ambush killings happened just two blocks from the scene of a similar murder last July when 18-year-old Donna Lauria was murdered while sitting in a car that was parked in front of her house. Since then, these seemingly connected attacks have left four dead and six injured."

"July, dude, since last July," Phil whispered under his breath like an impudent child.

Even though I was unfamiliar with the incidents, I was able to piece together what was going on. My original weird vibes from Silas that I had played off as nothing came crashing back into my memory. His reactions to the newscast, and his interactions with his people painted the picture of someone hiding in plain sight. Someone capable of vile and awful things. Someone with a power so strong and easily concealed.

Someone like me.

Candy continued. *"Lieutenant John Powers of the 8th homicide zone in New York said, 'There appears to be a direct link' between the fatal shootings yesterday of Valentina Suriani of 1950 Hutchinson River Parkway, Bronx, and Alexander Esau, of 352 West 46th Street. and the four previous ambushes. Attacking with no known motive or warning, police say the targets of the perpetrator seem to have common characteristics – young women with shoulder-length brown hair sitting in a parked car. Undoubtedly, this has cast a shadow of fear amongst the residents in the city that doesn't sleep."*

"Oh, they're all gonna go to sleep, alright!" John laughed.

"...A note from the murderer was also found at the scene of the crime, but detectives have yet to reveal its contents or relevance, if any, to the case. Police in New York are asking for any help with information concerning the .44 Caliber Killer."

Craig groaned obnoxiously and smashed the button of the television off. "Fucker!" he yelled.

"What the hell!" Phil sang. "Why didn't she say what was in the note?"

"They're not ready to say *'Son of Sam'*, I guess," John relented. "That sucks."

"Makes it too real," Craig said.

I digested it all. Took it all in. "So, all of that," I pointed to the TV. "You guys have something to do with that?" But I didn't need to play dumb. I already knew the score.

"Well, look who finally joined the party!" John exclaimed and the others laughed. Even Silas gave a small corner smile. "You said he was cool, Si. You sure about that?"

"The 22 Disciples of Hell, Silas," Craig added.

"Yeah, yeah, he's cool. He gets it. He's in. You're in, right Trent?"

I nodded. "For sure," but I shuddered on the inside at his words. They loomed in my head like a dark cloud waiting to explode into a monsoon.

"So, put the fucking jams on, why don't cha?" John said, and Silas pulled out a record from under the coffee table.

He set up the record player and before letting the needle descend on the plate, he handed me the sleeve.

I froze.

Dazed.

As if I had been taken out of this reality and transferred to another — transferred to another place and time. The three others melted away from my vision until it was just me, and Silas, and the record sleeve in my hand — the record sleeve with the black background and the rusty red letters written in an ominous font like dripping blood and bearing the name *Blodheksa*.

Blodheksa.

Silas gave me a knowing look. "You know them?"

It was a loaded question, and he must have sensed my dread and utter confusion. Something like the sound of rustling wings flittered in my head. Yes, I knew the word. I owned it. Lived it. Witnessed others die for it. It was the blood of my blood inscribed in ancient runes on yellowed paper, bound in leather, and carved inside a pentacle with a sacred stone. Six in existence — I knew where at least two of the original tomes were, but this? A record? My brain struggled to make the connection. I shook my head. "Never heard of them," I said, still dumbfounded.

"Oh, don't worry. I think you'll recognize it when it plays." Silas gave a head nod to Phil who laid the needle down.

The music started up as a rumble—a low frequency wave humming in the background that quickly grew to an ear-splitting crescendo, like a crash of thunder that was unexpected and rocked my insides to the core.

"They're from Norway. This album came out last year. New one coming out in October. They're getting pretty big in the underground scene."

Getting pretty big? As in, people are listening to this? I think, and Silas nods. I freeze again, contemplating the implications of a mass-produced version of the sacred text.

Unless, a name is just a name, and they're just a group trying to capitalize on some kind of theatrical angle.

Silas cranks up the volume, and the three others mindlessly cheer. "Wait 'til the vocals kick in. It'll blow your mind!"

And just as he said it, an explosion erupted in my skull as the words of the song made their way to my ears. Words that I knew. Words that I had spoken ages and ages ago. They came to me in my voice—my own, strong and confident voice—and in the voices of the old ones, and in the rune tattoos once burned on Blodwyn's skin, and in the painstaking task Aizel employed to create the saga, and so many other incidents and passages and events sweeping down violently through the annals of time. It awakened my memory and sharpened my senses. The music from the band syncopated with the music from the beyond and it played on and on—each spell, each teaching, each locked treasure opened all at once. The voice of the singer became the multi-layered voice of the eons. And when I closed my eyes and drifted with the sound, to the sound, I saw the tear in the sky start to open its mouth and glitter with stars and shine with the light of the absent moon. Genny howled again, and I knew just us three were privy to this wonder. Silas. Genny. Me.

The ones called Phil, John, and Craig were pretenders—underlings of a greater power set out to do its bidding. Mr. 44. Son of Sam. Whatever they called it. I looked to the left, and they all nodded their heads to the groove of the awful music, and I knew they couldn't hear it—they couldn't truly hear the multi-layered voices in their heads, couldn't truly feel the swoon in the pit of their souls. They were driven by something else, under the command and thrall of something beyond their own selves.

I blinked my eyes, and the music peeled back the veil so I could see. There in the living room, highlighted in red and orange tones, were Phil and John and Craig covered in blood. John held a knife, and the body of a dead dog lay in the center of a blood-drawn pentagram. In the present reality, Genny howled in agony. The others assumed the disjointed timbre of the music bothered her sensitive ears, but I knew she saw what I saw—the mutilated sacrifice of her baby brother, slaughtered on the night of a new moon, offered to the old ones to open the gateway and…

Slowly, ever so slowly and subtly, one voice rang out above the rest. It was a secret voice as if to only be heard by me, and it told me to be aware, be on guard. *There are others who would try to subvert our power for their own gain.*

I looked to Silas who stood gazing out the window. Did he see the rip in the sky? Did he see the burning trees in the distance and the gnarled limbs of the old ones turning and twisting their horrific bodies as they tried to descend upon our world? My inability to sense his presence from the start unnerved me and put me in a state of self-doubt. Was I losing my touch? Was I no longer an Aevir?

The music both inside and outside stopped, and Phil shut the record player off. Craig and John sat back down on the couch, and the three mused about the shootings in New York. Silas continued to glare out the window in deep thought.

"Blood witch," Silas said, his eyes trained on the street outside.

"What was that, Si?" Phil asked.

"Blood witch. Blodheksa. Blood witch."

"Yeah, man. That's what it's all about!" Craig said.

"What do you mean?" I asked tersely, and a hint of anger rose in my voice.

Phil moved next to the coffee table and sat on the floor. "The band. What they sing about. It's like a guideline or something. Like a handbook."

"How do you know what they're saying, though. It's not in English," I pried, trying to confirm my suspicions about the others.

Craig lit a cigarette. "Yeah, but Silas knows somehow. Don't ya, Si?"

Silas remained silent.

"So, what's a blood witch?" I urged.

"Only the most powerful witch in the world," Phil sang sarcastically, like I should have already known that.

But I did...

"Oh yeah, and what can this powerful witch do?"

"She's needed to open some kind of portal to hell. And whoever lets Satan out of the box will get eternal life," John joined in.

"That doesn't make sense. Wouldn't that be the witch? Wouldn't the Blodheksa be the one to get eternal life if she was the one to open the portal?"

"No, no, no," Craig corrected, "the Blodheksa doesn't open the portal. *Killing* the Blodheksa opens the portal."

Phil cracked open another beer in the kitchen. "So, who-ever kills the Blodheksa gets the prize."

My insides screamed at me, and a cold dread encompassed my body, but like Miss Candy Dobson from the news station, I forced myself to remain cool, calm, and collected. I snorted a little chuckle. "You have to find her first before you can kill her, though."

Silas turned from the window and cast his attention on me. His movement was slow and deliberate and as his head swiveled in my direction, I caught a glimpse of something around his neck glinting against the streetlight. A silver chain. I hadn't noticed it before. He pursed his bottom lip and sighed, "Of course, we're going to find her, Trent. We're going to find her, and you're going to help us."

Chapter Fifteen

Monday, April 18th 1977
Silas's House
Minot, North Dakota
Night of the New Moon

The night started to wind down. Phil had gone to one of the bedrooms off the side of the long hallway, John was passed out cold on the couch, and Craig slouched back in the armchair in a drunken, mumbling stupor. I sat on the floor, staring at the Blodheksa record sleeve, and contemplated my exit strategy. I had a lot to process and digest and getting back to my apartment was starting to look more and more like a viable and urgent recourse. Before I had the chance to make my way to the phone and call for a cab, Silas waved me over to come into the kitchen. "Come with me," he said. "I need to take Genesis outside. Let's walk."

I nodded and got up, and we exited from the back door and into Silas's wide-open backyard. The property was immense, and in the darkness, it looked as if it stretched for miles of flat land. I could faintly sense some trees rooting here and there out in the distance, but it wasn't a lush forest or anything like that. Genesis loved the space. Once she got outside, she took off running and bounded across the landscape like a misty apparition hovering above the grass. Her black body

was camouflaged with the cover of night, and the only time I caught a glimpse of her in the field was when she turned to look at us with her pale blue eyes. I reveled in watching her delight in her freedom for her spirit was truly one with the beyond.

"She's something special, isn't she?" Silas said, lighting a cigarette.

I nodded. "Sure is."

"I saved her. She was one of ten in her litter, and the others..." His voice trailed a little. "...I couldn't give her up. The second I held her in my arms, she looked up at me with those cool ass blue eyes, and I knew she was mine. We clicked, ya know?"

"She spoke to you."

Silas took a long, pensive drag. "You could say that."

"And the others? The others in her litter?"

He side-eyed me and continued to smoke.

"All of them were sacrificed," I said flatly, confirming what I had seen in my vision of Phil, John, and Craig.

"Pretty much," he answered, matter-of-factly. "That's why she's special. Saved. The beginning of all. Genesis."

At hearing her name, Genesis ran up to me, wagging her tail excitedly. I reached down to scratch the backs of her ears and she playfully licked my wrists and forearms whenever her tongue could meet my flesh. I stroked her coat from the top of her head down the length of her body, and her energy tingled through my hands like static electricity. Silas narrowed his eyes and huffed out a puff of cigarette smoke, obviously wary of my connection with his familiar. I gave her a final pat to her hind quarters and said, "Get," and she took off running again back into the darkness.

"So, tell me something, Trent. What all did you hear in the music?"

Instinctively, I bit my lower lip, stopping myself from saying anything. One thing was certain—I did not like the feeling coming from Silas, and I did not want to reveal my hand this early in the game. Because that was what it felt like—a game. A push and pull. Tug-of-war. A probing of the minds. "How much do you know?" "What do you feel?" "I'll show you mine, if you show me yours." I was uninterested. Unimpressed. Or at least that's how I needed to appear to feel. Besides, I'd played these types of games for centuries—I wasn't about to let this one slow me down or trip me up. Because I always won. Always. Even in the face of defeat, I always prevailed victorious. But I had to admit, this one was different. There were pieces on this chessboard that I didn't know how to move and...

"You play chess, Trent?" he said, breaking into my thoughts, and a wave of energy cemented me in place.

Okay, I thought. *If we're flexing our muscles...*

"Not a fan," I replied nonchalantly. "My dad tried to teach me once, but it never stuck. He did teach me a game called The Fox and the Geese. Ever hear of it?"

He inhaled his cigarette. "Nope. Can't say that I have."

"You play it on a chess board. It's an old game. Revolutionary War type of shit. So, one person is the fox, and the other person is the geese. There's only one piece for the fox on the board, but the geese have like thirteen pieces or something like that. Anyway, the object is, the fox needs to move around the board to catch the geese, and the geese need to move around the board to catch the fox, but the geese can only go forward, diagonal, or side to side. The fox, however..." I paused, breathed in heavily through my nose, and let the energy in my body build up. I clenched my fists and struggled to contain it—to hold it inside for a minute and let it pulse throughout my limbs. "...the fox can go anywhere he likes." I opened my hands and sent waves of energy into the cosmos like a beacon calling Genesis back to me. She sprinted to my side with her ears peaked at attention. She leaned back slightly on her hind legs and lowered her head in a defensive stance. Silas stared at her, and whatever commands he was trying to send, she ignored. A grumble rattled in her barrel chest, taking him off guard, putting him on high alert, but I closed my fist shut, and she immediately sat down on her haunches and panted happily as if being snapped out of attack mode and back to fun-loving Genny.

Trying to remain unfazed, Silas dropped the cigarette onto the ground, smashed it with his foot, and whistled through his teeth. Genesis perked up and trotted to the back door. "Let me show you something," he said, and I followed him.

Inside, he took me to a door that led to the cellar. He pulled a chain hanging from the pitched ceiling and a light popped on guiding us to the damp and dingy space below. It was cold in the basement—cold and wet with a strong mildewy smell that overpowered my senses. On one side of the room, the concrete walls were covered with maps of the United States— the kind you get from truck stops and post offices, which made sense to me considering the line of work Silas did. But the maps had markings on them—heavy red marker circles around different states, giant question marks in the corners of one, black X's furiously slashed through whole sections, arrows and notations pointing to certain areas. Like a jigsaw puzzle, or some kind of police detective board, the maps told a story that I was curious to hear about.

No, it's more like a treasure map.

On the other side of the room, the concrete walls were covered with drawings—rudimentary sketches of girls done in hard pressed pencil, some drawn meticulously and with great detail, others sketched with a frenetic hand. In every picture, the girl looked different, but there were similar features in each—shoulder length hair and overdrawn, exaggerated eyes. I perused the wall of faces and analyzed each one, trying to identify the source of their familiarity in my head. The drawings took me back to a time in my memory, and like the flick of a light switch, I recognized the eyes. They blazed with an intensity that could only resemble the one woman I knew who had the power of light.

Barbara.

My heart nearly stopped. It had been ages since we had seen each other, but I had always kept tabs on her whereabouts. She was an Aevir, like me, for I had made her that way so many years ago. Our time together was brief, but its power and importance left its mark through the centuries, and just like me, she had a significant role to play in the dawning of the blood witch. And there she was—replicas of her eyes pleading to me page after page, sketch after sketch.

"Who are these women?" I asked.

Silas stood at a workbench in the center of the room. "Wo*man*," he corrected. "I dream of her, get visions of her."

"You drew these?"

"Yeah. I had a great aunt who had been in a traveling circus. But she was like, the real deal. No fake bullshit. She told me how to manifest visions when I was a kid like it was a parlor trick or something. Called it scrying. My mom hated all that, though. Put a stop to it. Then she died. I don't know; I was so young. But I remembered the trick."

I walked over to him by the workbench. "And this is who you see? Who is she?"

"She's the Blodheksa. I know it. I can feel it. I just haven't gotten her down exactly."

Another map was spread out on top of the workbench. Unlike the others, this map of New York State had small red X's etched in a cluster on the area of Long Island, and an upside-down pentagram inscribed in blood to the north of the island. "Oh, Silas," I joked, "you never told me you taught geography in your spare time."

He snorted and shook his head with disdain. "You're a funny guy, Trent. That's how I knew you'd be a great addition to our group."

"The 22 Disciples of Hell?"

"Something like that."

"So, what's all this? Looks like you're tracking something down here." I circled the bench and inspected the map more closely. "Tracking something or looking for buried treasure." I clapped my hands with mock excitement. "Oh gee! You guys are secret pirates, aren't you? Under the guise of truckers, you cross the country in search of valuable booty."

He looked at me sharply. "Something like that," he answered, his voice lowering to an ominous octave.

I stopped in front of the map and zoned in on the red X's. I knew the area highlighted well, and I studied the pattern. Each red X had a number written in black next to it. "Bronx, Flushing, Floral Park, Flushing, Flushing," I read.

Silas slid up next to me, pushing me to the side. With a red marker, he drew another X in the Bronx section of the map and with a fine black pen wrote the number 6 inside a circle.

"And another Bronx," I said, admiring his handiwork. "The shootings."

He nodded. "I guess you can say it *is* a treasure map of sorts."

"What's the prize?"

He closed his eyes and inhaled with delight. "Paradise," he said on the breath out. "Tell me something, Trent. Have you ever felt like there was something *else*? Something *other*? Something beyond yourself? Something that you were drawn to, or more like *called* to? My whole life there's been this… this *knowing*. And I've searched for that something ever since I was a kid. Out there, around me, beyond me, in me… I've always felt like I was part of a larger design, a larger plan."

I knew exactly what he meant. I had seen so many others wrestle with the same quandaries as he did. I at least had the luxury of knowledge, but for fledgling practitioners, I had understood how difficult it could be to find their way. Some never did. Some never could. And I thought of all those that I had guided through the years, all those whom I served as a conduit. For *I* was the conduit—the driving force to introduce and guide the heksas from this plane of reality to the New Eden. *I* was the one to lead some of the most powerful heksas to realize their full potential and existence. Of course, there had been bumps along the way, and even times when I had forgotten my true purpose, but my search for the Blodheksa was the goal, it always had been, and always would be. Silas's revelation of his dark, longing soul made me want to reach out and embrace him as a brother. Made me want to scoop him up and take him under my wing, and say, "Yes! We will find the Blodheksa together! With me as the conduit and you as the shepherd, we will usher in the New Eden and open the gates to Paradise. Our Paradise!"

But I stopped myself when Aizel's voice and words from long ago came back to me, and drawings of Barbara's magic eyes stared at me from one side of the room: *Just because two beings walk amongst the dark doesn't mean they are kin.* I shuddered with her wisdom and remembered what Silas's crew had said before: they were trying to *kill* the Blodheksa, which was a concept directly misaligned with my own objective. "I think I understand," I lied, keeping myself concealed.

"I know you understand," he snapped. "I know you're pretending to be something you're not. And I don't mean like Craig, Phil, and John. It's the opposite. They're trying so hard to be disciples of hell, but you are an actual disciple trying hard not to be."

"Are *you* an actual disciple?" I sneered.

Silas glared at me for a few seconds then reached around his neck and tugged at the silver chain that had been hidden under his shirt. There was a pendant attached to it, fashioned similarly to my locust amulet—the one that held the ancient draugr and possessed much power, the one that rested comfortably in a wooden box in my apartment. My eyes widened and flashed with curiosity. He removed it and handed it to me, and I dangled it in front of my face, my eyes following it back and forth, back and forth. It radiated with a unique type of energy, like mine, but not quite the same. It was more muted in power, more subdued, and the pendant was much smaller than the one I had. Upon further inspection, it appeared to resemble an ant.

A child, I thought. *Too young of a human, too young of a draugr. It was easily extracted, and not powerful enough to put Silas in any real harm if he wears it often. Aizel must have been busy all those years after we parted. Between the books, and the babies, and the draugrs… there's no telling how many are out there in the wild.*

I clutched the pendant in my palm and drew the energy into me. Visions swirled in my head and fluttered behind my eyes, and Aizel's sweet voice hummed a tune—a familiar song that brought me back in time thousands of years, one she had often sang while she was deep in thought or focused on her work. I think I smiled at the memory, at the vision, and I caught the smell of her smoke-scented hair—the one she often had after hovering over her cauldron all day.

"Is she dead?" Silas asked.

I opened my eyes as a wave of shock crashed over me.

"The woman. I can hear her voice sometimes. She sings. Hums. You heard her, too. Just now. I know you did. It was written all over your face. I wonder who she is."

"She's dead," I said flatly. "She died a long time ago."

"The others can't hear her. What do you know about the necklace?"

"It's familiar, but..."

He sucked his teeth in with aggravation. He knew I was lying, and he held his hand out for me to return it. I gently placed it in his palm, and he snatched his hand away from me quickly, angrily. "Well, it's going to find the witch," he grumbled, and he held the necklace in the air, dangling the ant-like pendant above the map.

"What do you mean?"

"Watch," he said and as if on its own, the hunk of silver began to rotate. Silas was locked in position, as still as he could be. He extended his free arm above his head and drew down the energy from the new moon, pulling in the vibrations from the absolute darkness of the universe and filling himself with its energy. A translucent green light swirled around him, wrapping him in its tornado-like vortex. Like many witches throughout the ages, it was obvious he had mastered his own personal form of divination. The pendant spun around and around, slowly at first, then grew into a whirling frenzy until it froze it mid-air and leaned to one side. He lowered his arm and the vortex vanished into nothingness.

Silas looked down at the map, and with the tip of his pen, followed the space between the silver and the paper and made a small dot to where it seemed the pendant pointed. "Bayside," he said. "The next is in Bayside, Queens."

"The next killing?"

"Yes," he answered, putting the chain back around his neck.

"You're saying that's where the Blodheksa is?"

"It's not an exact science, but yes. It's in that general vicinity."

I leaned in to look closer at the map. Bayside. Flushing. Floral Park. Vicinity, but not. Not an exact science, indeed, but too close for comfort for my liking. There *was* a witch on Long Island—one of the best and brightest I had ever known. Barbara's light shone like fire in the darkest night. No, that's not right. She *was* fire incarnate come to cleanse this world. She *was* the Blodheksa once. Maybe she had finally found a way to regain that title? Either way, I knew I would have to protect her. I was her conduit once, once upon a time, and if there was a threat against her...

"When will it be done?" I asked, snapping out of my thoughts.

"Sometime next month. After the ritual of time."

"And who will carry it out? Will it be you?"

"Depends. Phil did the last one. This one could be Craig, or John, or our guy Dave in New York."

I shook my head in confusion. "Craig and John are false. You said it yourself. How would that work?"

Silas thoughtfully scratched the stubble on his chin. "Well, Trent, it really doesn't matter who does it—as long as it gets done in service to Him. Once the gates open, the demons will snuff out all the pretenders anyway, and only those like us will be allowed to remain."

"Those like us?" I questioned.

"You know what I mean, man. What's with you and the semantics, anyway?"

"And where do I fit in all of this?"

"I've got the 'where' down pat, and I'm pretty sure I've got the 'when' on my side. The only detail that's been fuzzy from the beginning is the 'who,' and that's where you come in, my friend."

"The 'who.' As in 'who is the Blodheksa.'"

"Yeah, Trent, not the rock band, that's for sure," he scoffed.

"Why me, though?"

"I saw it on you. I walked into Badlands, and you were sitting there at the bar drinking your drink, and when you turned around and looked toward the door, you had an X on your head. And I just knew."

I sighed. The necklace gave him the sight. That's how he could see me. And that's how he was going to locate the witch. *My witch.*

Barbara.

"Ever think maybe you're going about it the wrong way? Ever think there's an alternative to open the gates?"

"And what other way do you propose?" he sneered. "I know how to do this, Trent. I've studied for a long time."

Not as long as me.

"She's called the blood witch for a reason. 'Cause it's all about her blood. Spilling it. Dancing in it. It's the most powerful thing you've ever seen. The most powerful thing you could ever taste." He closed his eyes and smiled as if escaping to a sweet memory, and I started to wonder just how much experience he had with this way of life. "The songs on the record told me the story, and from what I can understand it all leads to the same outcome. She has to die. And you… well, I know you can help me figure out who the woman in the pictures is because the only thing keeping Sam from awakening is the lack of her blood."

"The Son of Sam?" I parroted back what I remembered one of the others saying earlier.

"No, Trent. Sam. Sam is the Devil. And I will make him come to heel. What do you say, man? Are you with me?"

I swallowed hard. Hesitantly. But I knew there was no other choice. I had to get close to him in order to gain and maintain his trust and stay one step ahead of him, and I needed to protect Barbara. I nodded, and he grinned.

"Great. We got a lot of work to do."

Chapter Sixteen

Friday, June 24th 1977
Silas's House
Minot, North Dakota
Night of the Half Moon

The more Silas's elaborate plan became clear to me, the more I knew I needed to shield myself from the group's wrath. I had fully understood that these 22 Disciples of Hell were nothing more than a ragtag group of misfits trying to bring peace and purpose into their lives. The only one with any true knowledge, or training, or power was Silas, and he ran the crew, made the plans, gave the orders, and kept all his little disciples in line while truly believing he would eventually open the gateway to hell.

Soon after the first night at Silas's, Craig, Phil, and John picked up their new jobs and went back out to work. Silas also had to get back on the road, so he asked if I would stay at his place and take care of Genesis for the few weeks he was gone. Normally, he would have taken her with him for company, but being that she and I had bonded, he figured I could just stay at his place with her, and in the meantime, I could figure out who the woman was. Little did he know, I didn't have to. I already knew, so instead of figuring out who she was, I spent my time figuring out how to keep her safe.

Silas was gone for the rest of April and all of May. The company he had taken a job with had run into some supply chain issues and that laid him up for some time in Wisconsin. Then there were mechanical problems on his rig as he headed into Ohio, and that became another holdup. Silas's two-week run turned into a four-week delay. He would call the house occasionally to check in—to see how Genny was and to see if I had made any progress. I would report back that everything was status quo and, no, I had yet to solve the case. I couldn't tell him outright that it was me who had sabotaged his latest work run, and that I had bonded so well with his dog that she wouldn't leave my side.

The .44 Caliber attacks had seemingly stopped because Silas was too preoccupied to give the orders. The last attack was in the middle of April, and when a few weeks had passed without incident, the people of New York probably sighed collectively thinking it was all over. But no such luck. When the media made an announcement that New York columnist Jimmy Breslin had received a letter from the Son of Sam, all hell broke loose again. The letter had said something to the effect that Sam was a thirsty lad, and the killings wouldn't stop until he had reached his fill of blood. This had caused Silas to freak out, as someone had gone over his head and sent the letter to the journalist without his approval. He had called the house screaming at me, "Did you do it? Who did this to me! What do you know?" And when I told him I was not involved and no idea who would do such a thing (I mean, I was in North freaking Dakota! What *could* I do from there?), he said, "Fuck this shit!" and slammed the phone down.

He was becoming undone. Unglued. It was obvious in his tone. And in a weird way, I understood that feeling. I knew what it was like to have that wanting, sinking, needing feeling in the pit of my stomach. I knew how it felt to have a raging storm building up inside my soul—just on the edge of exploding, but never getting to fully manifest itself. It hurt— both physically and mentally… emotionally. It was that fine line between confidence and self-doubt that could push a man over the edge with ultimate satisfaction or utter despair. There was no in between. And Silas felt he was so close, within reach of ultimate paradise, so he abandoned the job he had been delayed on, flew to New York to gather up some of the group, and came back home with renewed intent.

Earlier that day, Silas had instructed Genesis to catch a squirrel, which she obediently did. Daintily, she trotted the animal to the backdoor still alive in her teeth. Silas snatched it from her mouth by its tail, pinned its slender body to the countertop next to the kitchen sink, and chopped its head off. The blood poured into a Tupperware container, and when he was done, he gave the decapitated creature to Genesis to bring back outside. She flinched at the thing but did as she was told. He used the rodent blood to draw a pentagram on the cellar floor.

In the basement that night, I made it a point to wear and conceal the locust pendant during the ceremony so that I could cast a glamouring over the participants. With the pretenders in tow, I was prepared to throw them off the true track of the Blodheksa.

Black candles were lit and placed around the circle, and the five of us each took a seat at a particular point of the star. Silas sat legs folded at the north point with a drawing pad and pencil in his lap. I took my spot at the east point, John at the west. Phil was next to me at the southeast, and Craig at southwest. The New York map was sprawled out in the center of the pentagram, and a clear crystal was placed on the area that showed Bayside, Queens. Silas removed his pendant and handed it to me, then picked up the pencil. "Trent," he instructed, "hold the amulet over the crystal."

Phil opened his mouth to say something in protest, but Craig reached over and slapped his knee.

I forced the energy from Silas's pendant to flow up my hand and gather down into the silver that lay hidden against my chest to neutralize his control over it. The two essences slowly began to merge and the metal on my flesh got so hot I thought it would burn a hole right through me. Even if only temporarily, I would have complete control over Silas's pendant. The ant was easy to control, and I envisioned the two draugrs saying hello to each other as I pushed and pulled and stuffed them together in my mind's eye. I snickered at the silly thought, and the others eyed me sharply.

"Let's begin," Silas said. He put the pencil to the paper and began feverishly scribbling. I could feel his third eye widening at the center of his forehead and a surge of green light penetrating his inner vision. This was *his* manifestation of the power.

I dangled the pendant over the crystal and willed it to spin around over the mark on the map. With the ant draugr immersed in my locust, his sixth sense would not be able to read my mind or get snippets of my runaway visions. He would not be able to break into my head, even for a second, or hear the tail end of my thoughts. I was securely cloaked. And I was in complete control.

"Bayside, Bayside," Silas chanted, looking to the map then back to his sketch. "Where are you, my magic Queen?"

I forced the pendant to dance around as Silas pressed the pencil hard onto the paper. I closed my eyes and envisioned a girl—one with long brown hair and gentle eyes standing in a field of poppies with the summer breeze whipping through her hair. But it wasn't a summer breeze—it was a torrent of fire sweeping across the plains, scorching the flesh from the girl in the vision, making her countenance indescribable as she blew away to ashes into oblivion. Silas stopped his furious drawing, tilted his head, and closed his eyes, receiving my thought implant. "No, that can't be right," he muttered.

"Not Bayside?" John asked.

I forced the pendant to stop spinning and waver like a magnet over Bayside.

"No, I think Bayside is correct," Phil said.

"What's not right, Si?" Craig asked nervously.

Silas shifted and crinkled his face into a tight squeeze. I transferred my projection to him of a young girl with long brown hair dancing on the beach in a red swimsuit. The waves lapped at her toes as she let herself sink in the sand. But the waves weren't made of water, they were made of fire, and they burned the beach and the girl, so her face couldn't be seen, and her eyes couldn't be looked upon. She giggled wildly as she sank and burned, sank and burned...

Again, he tilted his head to the other side, trying to see and hear the vision more clearly. He was confused, unnerved, and his face strained with self-doubt and bewilderment.

"What's up, Si?" Craig asked with worry in his voice.

"I… I don't know," Silas stammered. "The face. The… the eyes. They… they changed."

Phil wrung his hands nervously. "What do you mean, they changed? How? How did they change?"

Silas ignored him and continued to draw, but he was perplexed, unhinged. His hand whipped across the page with wild strokes and long, crazy jagged lines. He turned the page over and wrote a series of numbers on the back and when he was done, he threw the pencil clear across the room. He tore the drawing from the pad and held it in front of his face for a minute, studying it. Then he turned it around to show us, and the three of them made a weird, collective hum of disapproval. The drawing looked as if it had been done by a child—a disjointed face with no discernable features, a stick figure body with a triangular dress to indicate a female, and flames for hair. Flames everywhere. Outside the figure, in the dress, all around. Flames. Flames to stop and consume even the most skilled heksa.

I sat quiet and still, and Silas snatched the pendant from my grip. The energy that had collected in the center of my chest was violently ripped out and pulled back into the ant. I couldn't help but gasp as he tore it away from me. He eyed my reaction with suspicion, and an alarm sounded in my head.

"Get our guy from New York on it, Craig" he said to the circle. "Two days. The coordinates are there."

Craig stood, took the paper from Silas, and walked upstairs. The others followed him, but Silas and I remained sitting in the circle for a long while, not saying a word to each other. What would happen in two days would be another failed attempt. And it would be a failed attempt because of me and my sabotage.

I knew it. Silas knew it. Silas knew I knew it. Silas knew *I* knew *he* knew it. So, we sat in an uneasy silence for what felt like forever. And in that moment of knowing, one thing was clear—Silas was going to make another attempt, and I was going to have to leave. Soon.

Saturday, July 16th 1977
The Thorne Residence
76 Rose Avenue
Franklin Square, New York
Afternoon of the New Moon

The sun blazed down at its apex in the perfectly blue sky. Not a cloud could be seen for miles of the horizon. A thin line of sweat formed where my forehead met my hairline, and I wondered if it was from the 91-degree heat that gripped the town, or if it was my own nerves getting the best of me. I surmised it was a little of both. I had gone to great lengths to get here – to track her down, evade detection within the cult, and of course, build up the courage to confront the woman I had abandoned almost three hundred years ago. I inhaled deeply at the thoughts:
How would she react to seeing me?
How would I react to seeing her?
Would she even receive me?
Believe me?
Panic set in at that thought—what if she didn't believe she was in danger? Then all of this would be for nothing…

I ran my sweaty palms down the side of my jeans. In the distance, I heard children laughing, but I shook the sound from my head and rang the bell. Within moments, someone from within bounded down the stairs, and the wooden door on the inside flung open. Behind the barrier of the black screen from the outer storm door, Barbara stood, glaring at me with legitimate confusion.

"H… hi," I stammered, like a silly little schoolboy unsure of himself.

"Um… hello," she replied. "Can I help you?"

I was at a loss for words. The cross-thatched design of the screen made her face look wild and jagged, but she was still my Barbara. Still, the brown-haired beauty with the magnetic eyes and perfectly pouted lips. She was still stunning, like time had barely had its way with her after all these years. Save for a shock of silver strands of hair at one side of her head, her alabaster skin was as smooth as it had been all those years ago.

And I saw her. Saw through her and into her. Saw passed the screen and the thick metal at the bottom half of the door. Saw into her soul and took comfort in the fires that burned there. They still burned. They still burned brightly and wildly. And the screams of all her victims still sung out against the smoke-filled sky with a beautiful song of torture and lamentation. And her children still laughed. *Our children*. The children who had been conceived of our passion, born, then put to the stake. Drowned in the fires of man. But did her fires still burn for me? As I stood there before her, her eyes were glazed with the ravages of time. Her memory bent and twisted. I feared she knew me not.

"Barbara?" I inquired. "Barbara Thorne?"

She brought her hand to her face and swiped back the side of her long hair over her shoulder. Her swift motion brought her scent wafting into my nostrils—the scent of sweet summer honey from the hive. I was mesmerized.

"Yes, that's me. What can I do for you?"

"Barbara *Flynn*?" I said in a low voice.

Suddenly, children's laughter echoed from up the stairs behind her. She darted her head to look up the long corridor staircase, then shifted her focus back to me with a confused look. But when our eyes met, it was as if she had awakened from a dream, and I knew.

She saw me. She knew me.

She remembered.

"It's not like I completely forgot, you know," she said, reading my thoughts.

"Oh yeah," I teased. "Then what is it?"

She smiled for a second, then her face fell harshly. "Protection. The memory of you was just too heavy."

"Oh, Barbara," I pleaded, "you know that…"

She opened the storm door that had separated us. "Come on in," she instructed. "It's hotter than hell out today! Besides, we have much to catch up on, don't we, lover?"

Chapter Seventeen

Saturday, July 16th 1977
The Thorne Residence
76 Rose Avenue
Franklin Square, New York
Afternoon of the New Moon

I followed Barbara closely up the long and narrow stairwell. Unlike my heavy footfalls that made the wood beneath me moan and creak, her gait was light and airy—it was as if she floated up the stairs to the small landing at the top. From the moment she opened the door to the apartment, I could feel her magic pulsating within. It was alive and breathing. Her energy hung heavy within the walls. There was a noticeable shift in the atmosphere—thick and restricting, almost like wading through a marshy swamp. It was obvious her power was deep and strong. *And controlled.* The last I had seen her, she was but a baby heksa herself—unsure of the full extent of her abilities, unsteady on her feet, yet ready to dive in. And now? She had grown exponentially, and I was amazed, though not surprised. In our brief time together, she had demonstrated the most promise. She had accomplished what so many other potential Blodheksas had not. *She was the one.*

In its hidden state, the apartment appeared like any other, belonging to your average American family. To the average eye,

there was a mother, a father, and two doting little ones who lived in this typical abode. But my second sight was able to see past the strong glamour—to see through the robust concealment. Like a wavy mirror at the circus, everything appeared to be in double. The perfectly laid out living room had a couch encased in plastic on an orange shag rug. Paintings of floral arrangements hung on the gold striped wallpaper, and a small bookcase next to the recliner housed New York Times Best Sellers like *Looking for Mr. Goodbar* and *The Moneychangers*. Even Barbara herself gave the vibe of a fashionable woman of the times wearing a black tank top and blue jeans that flared at the bottom. But it was all lies, because when the vantage point of the wavy mirror changed, I could see what was really happening beneath the surface—the demonic statue of the headless naked woman with the snake wrapped around her body, and the real painting of the lion at the circus with the person inside its mouth. The books on the shelf were certainly not New York Times Best Sellers—*Letters on Demonology* and the *Malleus Maleficarum*. I was pleased to also see *Blodheksa, Blodbrødre og Blodsøster* gracing the wooden shelf. I smiled at her beautifully crafted reality.

Hiding in plain sight...

A smaller hallway led from the kitchen to the back of the apartment. As I inspected the layout, I heard children's soft voices echoing from one of the rooms. I turned my head to her sharply and raised an eyebrow. The voices I heard before, and the voices I heard then? Could it mean the children were made flesh again? She motioned her hand for me to take a seat at the kitchen table and shook her head. "No," she said regretfully. "The children have not returned to me just yet."

I sighed. I knew all too well the feeling of needing to manifest something back into existence and not being able to. I knew the helplessness and hopelessness of defeat. I knew the utter despair and disappointment of being so close and having it slip away from my grasp time after time after time. "They are here, though," I said matter-of-factly. "They are always with you. They make themselves known and heard often and have kept you company all these years, haven't they?"

She sat down across from me and pulled her hair back into a ponytail. With a wave of her hand, the oppressive intensity of her house glamour lifted, and I breathed in a breath of relief. "Yes, but, to be made flesh..." her voice trailed. "Is that why you're here? Have you discovered a way to bring my children back?" She paused and held her breath. "*Our* children back?" she asked slowly on her exhale. For a second, hope shimmered in her black eyes, turning them to their natural honey brown. Like glitter reflecting back the light, they sparkled with wonder from the aura of my presence. Her body shifted forward with anticipation, and she folded her hands anxiously on the tabletop, but when I shook my head, it all melted away. Her eyes went dark again, losing that flickering light, and her shoulders stiffened up defensively. "Then why the hell have you come to me now?" she spat with venom. "To tell me things I already know?" She folded her arms across her chest. "Well, let me tell you something, Galen, or whatever the hell you're calling yourself these days... I'd be willing to bet there are things you need to hear from *me* right now!" She huffed a little, and I couldn't help but smirk. The fire inside her still burned wildly, and an odd sensation of pride warmed my heart.

"I'm Trent now," I said softly. "And I know we have a lot to catch up on, Barbara, but we don't have time for that."

Flames erupted in her pupils, and her energy rose through her from the bottom of her feet to her palms. The heat of her radiated through the wooden table, and for a split second I braced myself—feet planted onto the floor, hands gripped the edge. I readied myself to launch up and dodge her fiery attack. "We don't have time?" she asked rhetorically. "*We* don't have *time*?" she repeated, her voice and heat rising. "Isn't that *all* we have now, Galen? Isn't that the only thing left for us in this world? Time? And honestly, I don't care who you are now, you'll always be Galen."

The voices of the children in the back of the apartment suddenly stopped, like someone abruptly pulling a needle from a record. The door to their room creaked open slowly, and I craned my neck with hopeful anticipation to see if they would appear because I truly was curious to catch a glimpse of them. But the door shut with a thunderous *thud,* and I could not see anyone in the hallway. *But I could feel them.* Their ghostly presence rolled into the kitchen like early morning fog sweeping across the verdant plains. They hovered at my sides, then circled around—dark swirls of smoke surrounding me like threatening vultures. They were malice and menace and evil dancing in the air, causing me to feel conflicted. On the one hand, I was happy to be in their presence—to feel their strength and energy and realize that all three had grown so much and come so far. Yet on the other hand, their hostile intentions were palpable, and I needed to remain on guard—*regardless of kin.*

Barbara sensed my unease. She stood up, snapped her fingers, and dismissively said, "David. Gretchen. Enough." The fog gloom collected itself at the center of the table forming a thin line of black smoke that floated into the living room. It hovered over a blank canvas encased in a gold frame next to the lion painting. The smoke seemed to press itself into the black velvet background, as if it were burrowing its way into the surface. Within moments, the painted portrait of two children appeared—a boy and a girl with jet black hair and eyes like the blackest night dressed in suit and pinafore. Their pale faces stood out in stark contrast against the black velvet of the canvas and the darker tones of their hair and manner of dress. I squinted my eyes to get a better look from across the kitchen, and when I stared a little harder, they smiled back at me and giggled.

Barbara waved her hand again and they quieted down. "Speak," she commanded me. "For after all this time, I am curious to hear what has brought you back. Now. Here. Nowhere."

Her animosity struck me deep, but I couldn't blame her coldness toward me. Even still, I wanted to leap across the table, take her face in my hands and plant a thousand kisses across her lips and cheeks and eyelids. I wanted to pull her close to my chest and feel her blazing heat against my skin and explain why I had to leave her, why I had to let her go, and how very sorry I was for breaking her heart. But she would never have become the heksa who stood before me if I had stayed.

"The killings," I said. "The ones that have been happening recently."

She narrowed her eyes and looked at me as if I was crazy.

"You do know what I'm talking about, right?"

She put her hand on her hip and bounced on one leg. "I know," she snorted.

Sure, she knew. She felt it. She had hidden herself well with her strong glamours in order to protect herself—to take measures to ensure her safety. "Well, there's more to it. It's not as simple as random attacks. That's what the news people would have us believe, but it goes much deeper."

Her face twisted to the side, ear to the air so as to hear me, and *hear* me. "What do you mean?" she asked, and then the reality of it hit her like a ton of bricks that came crashing down on her face. Gone was her sarcastic and icy demeanor, replaced with one of apprehension. "Wait a second. How did you find me?" Her voice was slow and quiet.

I stood up and walked over to her, and her shoulders tensed up when I got close. "It's okay," I coaxed and removed the locust pendant from my neck, dangling it before her.

Her eyes widened, glowed, changed from black to brown to a bright, blazing red. The flames within them danced fiercely, like hot thin columns rising up to the heavens. A low-sounding drum beat in the distance and a chorus of muffled voices rose up in a discordant song. The children in the picture giggled again.

Barbara cupped her hands beneath the silver amulet. An orb of light formed in the center of her palms as she pulled out some of the necklace's power and absorbed it back into her, like someone dying of thirst greedily drinking from a fountain. The light crept up her arms, illuminating her skin from within, and raced its way to the center of her chest. She breathed heavily when it reached her center, and her eyes fluttered with pleasure when it was fully incorporated inside. "Where did you? How did you?" she stammered breathlessly, swooning from the aftereffects. "My necklace…"

"It found me. And that is how I found you." I dropped the necklace gingerly in her hands and a wave of static electricity needled my fingertips. "But it's also the tool he's using to find you."

She looped the chain around her neck and held the medallion out in front of her, beaming with happiness like a child who found a lost treasure, or more like a parent being reunited with a lost child. I thought I heard a low gasp come from the painting, and when I looked over at it, the children's mouths were dropped open with surprise. "What do you mean?" she asked, her eyes still trained on the heavy silver amulet.

"There's another pendant. Another necklace."

She clutched it tightly to her chest and closed her eyes. "Six," she whispered.

"Huh?"

"Nothing. Continue."

"The person who has it is using it to find someone. The Blodheksa. The witch with the most powerful blood. He thinks that killing you will..."

"Open the portal," she interrupted. "But he's so very wrong, isn't he? That's not the right way."

"I'm not one hundred percent sure of it. He and his group are certain their way will complete the path. I can't rule out the possibility that *our* way and *their* way would both suffice in getting it done."

"And just because there are others out there like us, doesn't mean they are *like* us. There are others who would try to subvert our power for their own gain," Barbara sang, but it was Aizel's voice that rang clear. I paused for neither I nor Aizel had ever spoken those words to her.

Yet she heard.

"But that's just the thing," I continued. "He's not like us. Not entirely. We have one thing he doesn't."

"Time?"

"Exactly. We are Aevir, the Eternal. He is not. Nor are those under his command. He can't fully control the power of the pendant and what lies inside it. He has some understanding of what it can do, but he doesn't know the actual extent of it. Only we can release that power."

"I can control it," she asserted in a faraway voice.

She sat down at the table, still holding the amulet close, still clutching it so tightly as if she would never have let it go. "His," she said after a minute of contemplation. "How did he come to be in possession of it?"

"I don't know for sure. It doesn't really matter, though. The fact is, he has it. It's much smaller than yours, and its power is not as pronounced, but it's somehow connected to you, Barbara."

"And Blodwyn," she whispered, but I ignored her and continued.

"He's been using it as a tracker. And while it's not exact, he and his people are getting closer. They call themselves the 22 Disciples of Hell, and I suspect they might be part of a larger organization. The point is, they are attacking these women on his orders. He performs a ritual inside a bloody pentagram and uses the pendant to divine the information—the where, the when, and then the *who* in the form of a drawing. For the last year, he's tried to construct a composite of you. He then gives these drawings to his underlings so that they can conduct the attacks in hopes of opening the gates. The last time he did the ritual, I intervened and muddled the visions, but he sensed my interference right away. He knows too much and is too deeply connected. You've done well to conceal yourself, but he's coming."

"Silas," she breathed.

I paused again, marveling at her blossomed strength.

"Yes, Silas."

"Brunette, medium-length hair. Parked car. Late at night," she said the descriptors like Candy Dobson had that night on the newscast.

I nodded, and with that, Barbara raised her palms about two inches from her face and moved her hands up and over, to the top of her head and down the length of her black ponytail. Magically, in its place, blue eyes peered out at me, and a mane of blonde locks replaced her silver-shocked hair.

"That should confuse him for a bit," she cooed.

I smiled at her glamour. "For a bit. You've done very well for yourself," I commended.

"Well," she shrugged, "there's still much to learn. Having to teach myself has been an experience, to say the least. It would have been much easier if I had some kind of guidance..."

"Barbara," I said apologetically, placing my hand on her bare shoulder. The heat of her skin would have burned a normal person, but I let her fire radiate in me and through me.

"Forget it," she said, pulling away from my touch. "Maybe we can talk about everything when this is all over. Or maybe not. How long has it been, actually? 280? Yet you feel so close. So... familiar. Like you were never gone. Like time..."

"Never passed," I finished her thought.

She smiled half-heartedly, remembering the nights we spent lazily in each other's arms, speaking to each other only through our thoughts.

"I surmise you'll be staying here?"

"Just until..."

"The threat is eliminated? We'll have to go our separate paths once more?"

"Something like that," I sighed.

"Fine," she said with authority. "Just as long as we're both on the same page with how this is going to work 'cause I'm over surprises, and I prefer to know ahead of time what I'm dealing with."

Chapter Eighteen

Thursday, August 4th 1977
The Thorne Residence
76 Rose Avenue
Franklin Square, New York
Night of the Waning Gibbous Moon

When news broke of another attack, Barbara and I weren't too concerned at first. But as the details rolled in, it was clear that she was in more danger than we had originally thought. Robert Violante and Stacy Moskowitz were ambushed in Brooklyn in similar fashion to the other victims; however, this attack was different for the fact that Stacy was a blonde—the first and only blonde to have been targeted. Since I arrived in Franklin Square, Barbara had remained behind the locust glamour as fair-headed, which made our daily interactions interesting, to say the least. She had changed so much in her demeanor and confidence that I scarcely recognized her at all, and with the extra layer of the camouflage surrounding her, it was like being with a completely different person. But her aura was still the same, and glints of the old Barbara often shone through and stirred up the old memories and feelings I had of her. Yet, in the days of our reunion, we had not rekindled the passion we had once shared. I was disappointed,

but in a strange way, I understood—Barbara was still scarred from our separation.

And then Stacy Moskowitz died and something like a groan shuddered within the walls of Barbara's apartment. And that could only mean one thing—*Silas was close.*

Or most likely, Silas was *here.*

Barbara sprawled out on the couch, and I sat cross-legged on the floor watching the television on the opposite side of the room. "I'm next, aren't I," Barbara said flatly when the news program ended.

I nodded slowly, for we both knew the inevitability of the situation. Barbara curled up in the fetal position on the side of the couch, buried her face into the pillow and sighed. It was unnerving to see her wallow in the face of defeat. "Don't worry," I encouraged. "We'll figure out something." She sighed again.

I looked up to the painting of the children and the little girl had covered her face within the crook of her brother's shoulder, mimicking Barbara's actions. The boy wrapped his arm around his sister's back and brought her in close to him. A single tear crept from the side of his eye, and his frown was vastly exaggerated. A strange feeling overcame me as I had the sudden urge to comfort all three of them at once— my sweet Barbara, whose former fragility had returned, and Gretchen and David, the spirit children whose faces mani- fested in oils and velvet and translucent black smoke.

I ran all the possible scenarios and possible outcomes in my head—ones of us running away and living under the con- stant veil of concealment. It was possible that Silas could lose our trail and give up altogether, or he could run out his own mortal clock and eventually die. But those were such drastic measures, and honestly, I wasn't interested in spending the last part of the century in hiding.

Barbara's bookshelf was directly underneath the chil- dren's portrait, and my eyes glanced over the collection of books that laid within. Suddenly, a wickedly delicious idea overtook me, and I looked up at the children and smiled wide. David shook Gretchen's arm and wisps of their black smoke circled around the frame and descended over me. It tickled as they hummed by my ears and wrapped themselves around my neck and on top of my head like a ghostly hat. They fished in my brain, much like Aizel used to do, and once my idea was made known to them, the last of the smoke traveled back into the portrait, bringing life to their faces again. Gretchen turned her head to me with her mouth agape and eyes wide. David's face washed over with relief, and the two hugged with joy.

Sensing the atmosphere shift in the room, Barbara's head shot up from the pillow and her eyes narrowed with curiosity. "What just happened?" she demanded, scanning the portrait like a defensive mother inquiring about her children. "What did you say to them?"

I chuckled. "I didn't *say* anything!"

The two in the painting raised their hands to their faces and a faint giggle echoed in the living room.

"Har har, don't play semantics with me, Galen. You clearly did something for them to react like that."

"Do you have a map of Long Island?"

"What? What are you talking about?"

"Do you have a map of Long Island?" I repeated calmly. "Or New York. Yeah, better if you had a map of the whole state."

She got up from the couch and glided into the kitchen. "I probably do in the junk drawer somewhere. Why? What are you thinking?"

I reached over to the shelf, pulled the *Blodheksa* book out and placed it on the rug. "We're going to draw him out," I said confidently. "I know how he does it, and with the two of us working together, I'm sure we can get a fix on his exact location."

"He's powerful, though. He controls the essence of a pendant, you said it yourself! And he has his army—his disciples. He'll see it coming. He'll know we're tracking him."

"Good. Let him know. Let him come."

She rummaged through the top drawer of the kitchen cabinets and tossed take-out menus and notes scribbled on yellow-lined legal pad paper onto the floor until she finally found a wrinkled-up map of the Tri-State area. "This is all I got. This'll have to do."

"Perfect," I smiled and waved her over to me. "Come. Sit. Take off the necklace."

Barbara paused and took a step back in hesitation. "B… but if I take it off…"

"So what?" I interjected. "The glamour disappears. Yes. You remember how it works. Jeez, has it been *that* long?" I teased, trying to ease her apprehension.

She knelt across from me and smoothed the map out on the floor, but her expression was still wrought with doubt. Cautiously, she removed the chain from around her neck and as it looped over her face, her true visage manifested before me like an ocean wave crashing onto the sandy beach and sucking itself back into the sea. Her black hair fell about her shoulders, silver-streaked with shocks of pure lightning racing through the strands. Her dark eyes sparkled with a fearful, yet innocent look that hypnotized me and brought me back to centuries passed with a feeling of warmth and light in my heart. Though she was fully clothed, she felt naked in front of me, in her true form, and I soon understood that her apprehension of taking off the necklace and breaking the glamour had more to do with me than with Silas. She was vulnerable as old feelings stirred wildly inside her and a rush of pink invaded her cheeks.

"It's okay," I coaxed. "I'll keep you safe. I promise."

Her face darkened with embarrassment. "I don't need you to keep me safe."

"I know," I whispered and leaned over the map. "But I will do it anyway."

More children giggles echoed faintly in the room, and from the corner of my eye, they had innocently covered their eyes with their hands. I smirked at their playfulness and reached in to kiss Barbara softly on her forehead. *Don't worry, I'm being nice with your mother,* I said to them in my mind. Barbara heard it, too. She huffed a little laugh, and we both sat down on the rug.

"Shall we?" she asked, tilting her head and dangling the necklace over the map.

I opened the book and reached for her free hand. "No time like the present."

I always loved the way the book sounded when invoked. The music of it was ancient and dissonant, a cacophony of disharmonious voices and rudimentary instruments. And at that moment, I understood why that rock band had chosen that style of music to transfer the spells onto—it was only in the harshness of the crude instruments and the disjointedness of the ensemble that the true words of the old ones could be discerned. Who they were and how they had come into possession and transference of the *Blodheksa* text was beyond my knowledge, and I knew I would have to save that investigation for another time...

The drums started low. It was always about the drums! There was always something soothing in the lull of it all, something spellbinding and hypnotic. As soon as the book was turned open, I knew Barbara felt it, too. She squeezed my hand tight when it hit the center of her core. The fire ignited within her at once and sent a shock of heat up my arm and into my chest. The pendant swung around and around over the map, and I spoke on the inside with a gravelly, archaic voice – conjuring the draugr, and the power, and the great beyond to do my will.

Our will.

And there, the air around us shifted, the apartment walls melted away, and music of the book lifted us to a forest—a vast field of silver-branched trees under a dome of the star-studded sky. Barbara smiled at me, and I embraced her and burrowed my head in the crook of her neck. The scent of her smoky hair filled my senses and I covered her with a thousand kisses—short and quick pecks up and down her neck, to her cheeks, up the side of her face, across her forehead and back down to her lips where I locked onto her mouth with a fury of passionate kisses. She swooned in my arms, her body went limp, and she arched her back when I pulled her in closer. The heat coming from between her legs radiated against my knee. *She'll burn me alive,* I thought. But I didn't care. I wanted her to. I wanted her flames to burn through and consume me. I wanted to plunge into her sex with my tongue, and fingers, and cock, and let her fire disintegrate every last fiber of my being. I reached one hand up her sundress, cupped her crevice, and pressed my thumb gently against her flesh. She squealed through our kisses and wiggled her body against the pulse of my finger. I opened my eyes and looked up to see a tear in the sky had formed with tiny glittering stars filtering down like confetti exploding from a popped balloon.

They fizzled into puffs of hissing white smoke when they touched her shoulders. She pulled away from my kiss and touch and threw her head about in a circle, admiring the gash in the sky, admiring the falling stars. "Not now," she cooed. "We have other business to attend to."

I grasped her hand, and we went walking through the woods. The forest was deep and wide and unfamiliar. The menacing limbs of every tree dipped down low, almost brushing against the tops of our heads. They bowed to us, granting us access into their domain, and positioned their branches to point us in the right direction. We came upon a section of trees surrounded by a mass of piled up leaves. A burned-out fire smoldered next to it and a buzzing noise echoed throughout space. Flies danced in the air and around the leaves and sang their ominous song of murder and chaos. Death was all around us. I felt it looming in the darkness with its blanket of decay. I tasted it on the roof of my mouth when I breathed in through my nostrils. Barbara picked up a stick and prodded the heap of leaves. "I've seen this before," she said. "I've been here before."

"There's a body underneath, isn't there?" I said.

"Yes. But this hasn't happened yet."

Her voice was angelic, bell-like. It rang out above the jarring din of the song of the old ones.

The wind blew up again and a voice spoke to me from the trees: *An unfinished dissection of flesh. A mass of unrecognizable decomposition. He screamed a thousand times.*

In my mind's eye, I pulled up everything I remembered about Silas. Silas Creed. Short, black hair Silas. Scarred face Silas. Everything I could recall of his stature and essence. His voice, his demeanor, his mannerisms, his quirks. The image of him started out as a drawing, much like the women on his basement walls. I scribbled each fine detail of him plucked from my memory onto a piece of astral paper and waved it in the last remnants of the sputtered stardust. "Look," I commanded Barbara and held the paper up to her face. She absorbed his countenance and said his name out loud. "Silas," she hummed, closing her eyes.

"Remember, words are spells," I cautioned.

"Our spell," she replied, and when she opened her eyes, they were blazing red. A shadowy outline of a man appeared next to the dead body.

Silas.

A crow flew onto one of the low-hanging branches of the trees. It too had piercing red eyes that glowed in the twilight of the forest. Its black feathers shimmered iridescent like an oil slick hitting the sunlight and reflecting back greens and yellows and purples and golds. "I think I know her, too," Barbara said pointing to the bird.

"I do, as well."

The crow cawed, and in its voice, it said, "You are death."

"I am death," Barbara repeated.

"We are death," I reinforced.

With one last shrill cry, the crow flew over to the figure of the man and plucked his eyes from his face. The man screamed in agony, but he soon faded away from our vision and the sound of his screams was replaced by a new one. Not the buzzing of the flies or the ancient drums or the songs of the old gods or the guttural voices of the collective Legion. This sound grew softly at first then took over the background essence of the forest, rising to a loud, incessant chirp. Not a bird chirp, but more of a grinding sound that resonated in the air. A harsh strained sound rose up from the soil and from deep in the hearts of the trees.

The paper-thin cry of the locust.

"That's funny," Barbara said gripping the pendant. "The locusts aren't due back for seven more years. Yet here they are. At your command."

I raised a hand in the air, and a black swarm gathered high above us, blacking out the light from the stars and the bulge of the waning moon. Their sound crescendoed to a wailing, bleating sound, and when I lowered my arm back to my side, they quieted and dissipated back amongst the trees.

Barbara closed her eyes and tugged at the chain. "We can go back now," she smiled.

In the apartment, we unlocked our hands. The music stopped and we both stared as the pendant hovered over a spot on the map. "Yonkers?" she said, crinkling up her nose. "Why would he be in Yonkers?"

"That's where he is. That's where he'll be waiting for us."

"You mean me."

"Yes, Barbara. He's there waiting for you."

Friday, August 5th 1977
Untermyer Park
Yonkers, New York
Night of the Waning Gibbous Moon

Barbara and I arrived at the park close to 11:00 p.m. Its massive grounds sprawled out for miles, and for the average person, trying to find someone would have been near impossible. But we were not average people, and we were not trying to find just anyone. Using the image of Silas that I had implanted in her mind, Barbara drew from the energy of the locust and based our steps on the vibrations from within. Silas made our search that much easier as he used his amulet to draw us in, just as much as we were using ours to guide us to him. It was a push and pull of a dance to unite the two powers. It was almost as if the draugrs were calling to one another.

We stopped suddenly and stared at each other when we reached an abandoned gatehouse. A pulse rushed through us both at the same time and a low rumble rose up from the ground. The crumbling stone structure had graffiti spray-painted on the outside walls, and two ominous lion statues guarded the opening like two aged sentries frozen in time. Barbara walked up to the stone doorway and peered her head inside as I took a step back to conceal myself within the trees. The clouds covered the entire sky, giving no sign of the stars or moon above, and I got a sick feeling in the pit of my stomach that something wasn't right. Something was off. I could feel it in the air—the thickness of it, the heaviness in my chest, the metallic scent wafting in the air. It made me unsettled.

Before Barbara could step foot into the structure, Silas appeared from the opposite side. He manifested out of what seemed like thin air, surprising even me with his stealthy entrance. Barbara spun around on her heels and clutched the pendant at her neck.

"Hello," he said to her in a kind voice.

"Hello," she acknowledged back sweetly.

"You know you're standing on the threshold of hell, don't you? Literally."

Barbara looked about her with frantic eyes, and at the exact same time as she did, I noticed it as well. In front of the stone opening of the gatehouse, a fresh pentagram was drawn in blood. It was large, and when I took a step forward to get a better look from my vantage point, the tip of my shoe knocked into something on the forest floor. I looked down and at my feet was the corpse of a decapitated German Shepherd. *Genesis?* My heart sank.

"We haven't met," she said nonchalantly, mustering every ounce of calm within her soul.

"No, but I believe we have a mutual acquaintance. Trent? He's somewhere around here, isn't he?" Silas chuckled.

Barbara ignored him and tried to move gingerly away from the pentagram, but a clicking noise and a low growl stopped her dead in her tracks. "No, no, that's quite alright," he said. He raised his arm at his waist, revealing his .44 revolver as Genny sauntered to his side. I sighed with relief that he had not mutilated her.

Barbara froze and clutched her pendant tighter. She tried calling out to me in her mind, but Silas's energy muffled the sounds. *It's okay, Barbara,* I said to her. Silas smirked and sniffed the air like Genny did when she sensed something. "Barbara?" he questioned with the tilt of his head.

She didn't respond.

"It's been over a year, Barbara. I've been looking for you my whole life, actually. I just didn't know it."

"Well," she said, the nervousness creeping its way into her soft voice, "seems we found each other, doesn't it?"

He took a step forward, but the gun remained at his side. "Me more than you, though. We're the same, you and I. And Trent, too, but once I realized he was protecting the Blodheksa rather than helping me get to her, that was a game changer for me."

"I'm not the Blodheksa anymore," she said with conviction. "I don't think you have the slightest idea what that means."

Silas made a condescending *tsk* sound in his mouth. "I beg to differ," he sneered.

Genny growled again, so I stamped my foot hard on the ground snapping some branches. Just as I had suspected, her ears perked up, and she left Silas's side to investigate the noise. Silas and Barbara continued to have their villain versus antihero dialogue, and I barely tuned in to their exchange. Genesis came sniffing around the tree I was hidden behind, and when she looked up from the base and our eyes met, her tail went wild, and she jumped on me with excitement. Her head in line with mine, I nuzzled her and whispered, "Good girl. I missed you, girl. You're such a good girl. Easy, easy." She plopped down back on all fours, and I bent down beside her stroking her fur and patting down her underbelly.

I'm here to protect that one. I said to her, and she licked my face in acknowledgment. *I can save you now, too. You know the truth, Genesis. You are the truth, Genesis. The truth, and the light, and the way. You will serve me, won't you, girl? For you have seen the shift in the sky, haven't you?*

She panted and furiously wagged her tail. The energy inside her took over and the entire length of her body became electric. Like she was kissed by lightning, as Barbara had been. We both crouched down low and waited for a signal, any signal, for us to make our move.

"Galen!" Barbara screamed, and I shot up at attention. Silas had somehow paralyzed her in place and had crept up behind her with the gun pressed up against her temple. Genny growled again, but I raised my hand to hush her and stepped out from behind the tree so Barbara could see me.

Still, the scene felt off. To the naked, normal eye, Silas had Barbara dead to rights. He would carry out his goal, spill her blood in the circle and open the gateway for the old gods. But this was *Barbara*. Barbara of the Red Thorn. Mother of the Twins. Consort of the Conduit. The reformation of Blodwyn, the most powerful heksa I had ever known.

There was no way that...

I smelled the burning before I could say a word. Silas released her from his hold and jolted back, swatting at the fire that burned the front of his shirt. "What the fuck?" he screamed.

Genesis barked, and the fire in Barbara's eyes got brighter. She smiled at me, and suddenly the song of the locusts in the woods circled around us.

"Go," I commanded my familiar, and Genesis dashed over and clamped her strong jaw around Silas's ankle. She pulled him down and dragged his body to the center of the circle. Silas screamed and cursed and tried to fight her off, but I used my own strength and will to hold him down. Barbara bent over, removed the chain from around his neck, and looped it around hers. A metallic *clang* sound resonated when the two pendants touched, and she inhaled deeply with a new surge of power.

"He's yours," she said to me.

"Mine?"

"A long time ago, you gave me someone to do what I wanted with. Consider this a gift returned."

I raised my hand, and the locust chirps grew louder, and Genny's bite went deeper, and Silas's horrific cries got more frantic.

"Oh no, my love. This is all you," I said, and Genesis backed up and over to my side.

Barbara nodded, and with ease and grace and the daintiest of gestures, she lit him up. It was a glorious sight to behold as he lay there in the circle, motionless and screaming against the roar of the flames. Her enchanted fire burned yellow, to orange, to red, to black in one of the most marvelous spectacles the human eye could behold. Genesis cowered behind me and groaned. I pet her to reassure her she was safe.

We stayed until Silas no longer screamed, and all that was left was a pile of ash and fragments of bone, and Barbara knelt over the hot remains, ground her hands into what was left of him and made imprints up and down her bare arms.

Saturday, August 6th 1977
The Thorne Residence
76 Rose Avenue
Franklin Square, New York
Morning of the Night of the Half Moon

"Will it be centuries before our paths cross again?" Barbara asked woefully as we stood in the threshold of the front door.

I shrugged, but the agony of having to leave her again struck me deep. "Take good care of her," I said nodding my head up the stairs. Genesis howled from the landing and Barbara smiled.

"I will."

"She'll protect you."

Barbara sighed. "You know I don't need protecting."

"No. I suppose you don't." I smiled back.

"The attacks will stop now that he's gone. The group will put a fall guy up and that'll be that."

I remembered what Silas's group had said. "Yeah. They have a guy from Brooklyn that they didn't think too highly of. I bet it'll be him. He's the easiest one to nab."

"The Son of Sam," she mused.

"The Son of Sam," I repeated.

"Who is Sam anyway?" she laughed

I shrugged. "According to the 22 Disciples, Sam is the devil, so…"

She stepped closer to me and put her hands on my shoulders. "They had it wrong," she said staring deeply into my eyes. They changed their color to an ice blue, like Silas's, like Genny's, and I did a double take. Light from the two pendants around her neck caught the morning sunlight and made me blink. By the time my eyes came back into focus, her eyes were back to their deep brown hue.

You have it all wrong, she said on the inside. Her voice was harsh and guttural, like a chainsaw grinding against metal.

It felt as if the world stopped spinning as my mouth opened with shock. "W… what do you mean?" I stammered.

"A host. A legion. Not just one to open the gates. I've seen that special place, Galen. In my darkest dreams, you find me there. But we can't get there without the others."

"Yes, Barbara. The three. The Blodheksa, The Blodbrødre and the Blodsøster."

"No, Trent!" she exclaimed, taking me off guard. "There are others. I know it. I feel it. The draugrs told me."

"I don't understand! What do you mean?" I yelled, trying to keep my composure.

"A host of ten. The Three and The Conduit, The Shepherd, The Oracle, The Scribe, The Crone…" she paused as if she were scanning her mind for the others. "I… I don't know. That's all I heard. But there are ten. Ten to bring forth the old ones. Ten to bring about the New Eden."

I sighed. "And we still have different paths to go until that can happen."

She nodded and kissed me on the cheek. "Stay with me," she whispered through a knot in her throat.

"Be not afraid. I go before you always."

She looked up as tears escaped from each of her eyes. "I'll be leaving this place soon. Come with me."

I wiped her cheek with my thumb and kissed her lips gently. "I can't. You know I can't. I think I'm going to stay in New York for a little while. There are forests and trees out east that call my name."

"Always you and that Black Wood," she chuckled and rolled her eyes.

I laughed, too. "Yeah. Besides, you said the locusts are due to come back in seven years?"

"Yes. '84."

"'84, eh? That feels like a good year."

"A good year for a locust?" she asked.

"A good year for a Silver Locust," I corrected and sent her images of us dancing naked under the burning red sky blanketed with a swarm of locusts in the New Eden. Our new world. A time and space where we could be together with our brethren in a world just for us. Where evil and malice weren't deemed so—where we could revel in the pleasures of our deepest, darkest desires. *And dreams.* In my vision, Barbara's long black hair with shards of lightning held a crown of red thorns atop her head, and we sway to the sounds of the old ones as they devour the world. *You hear them, my love,* I say into her mind. *We are there forever.*

"You are the Silver Locust," she whispered into my ear.

"I am the Witch of the Silver Locust," I whispered back and gave her a parting kiss.

Book Club Questions

1. Trent is not the Blodheksa, but he is connected to her. Explain the role of the Blodheksa in Trent's story.

2. Were there any scenes that stood out to you? If so, why?

3. If you have read any of the other books in the series, how was this similar or different to the others?

4. Explain the importance of the silver locust necklace. How does it impact the trajectory of Trent's life as well as that of the Blodheksa? And why a locust instead of something else? How is the locust symbolic regarding the long-term goals always looming over Trent?

5. What growth do you see in Trent throughout the book?

6. Sexual encounters are intertwined with Trent's other experiences. How is sex important in Trent's journey as well as the opening of the portal?

7. How does Trent's relationship with Barbara compare with his relationships with Poppy and Aizel?

8. Discuss Chris and the Church of Satan. How was this an important stop in Trent's journey, even though the outcome may not have been what he had hoped for?

9. Consider the various settings of the book (Early Civilization, 1966 California, 1977 North Dakota, 1977 New York). Is there any significance to them? Would you have picked different settings if you could, and why?

10. How would you describe the energy around Silas? How does his energy impact that of Trent?

11. Discuss the Son of Sam plotline. What are your thoughts on it, given the real-life nature of it? How did it impact the fictional plot of the book? Did it change your views of the story at all?

12. What are three adjectives you would use to describe Trent? Why?

13. Trent states repeatedly that his life's purpose is to restore the Blodheksa. Do you feel this is accurate or is there anything underlying that he may not have unpacked yet?

14. Witches are often portrayed as female. How has Trent's role as a witch impacted your view of the archetype?

Author Bio:

Maria DeVivo writes horror and dark fantasy for both a YA and an adult audience. Each of her series has been Amazon best-sellers and has won multiple awards since 2012. When not writing, she teaches Language Arts and Journalism to middle school students in Florida. A lover of all things dark and demented, the worlds she creates are fantastical and immersive. Get swept away in the lands of elves, zombies, angels, demons, and witches (but not all in the same place). Maria takes great pleasure in warping the comfort factor in her readers' minds—just when you think you've reached a safe space in her stories, she snaps you back into her twisted reality.

MORE BOOKS FROM
4 HORSEMEN PUBLICATIONS

FANTASY, SCIFI, &
PARANORMAL ROMANCE

AMANDA FASCIANO
Waking Up Dead
Dead Vessel

BEAU LAKE
The Beast Beside Me
The Beast Within Me
Taming the Beast: Novella
The Beast After Me
Charming the Beast: Novella
The Beast Like Me
An Eye for Emeralds
Swimming in Sapphires
Pining for Pearls

CHELSEA BURTON DUNN
By Moonlight

DANIELLE ORSINO
Locked Out of Heaven
Thine Eyes of Mercy
From the Ashes
Kingdom Come
Fire, Ice, Acid, & Heart
A Fae is Done

J.M. PAQUETTE
Klauden's Ring
Solyn's Body
The Inbetween
Hannah's Heart
Call Me Forth
Invite Me In
Keep Me Close

JESSICA SALINA
Not My Time

KAIT DISNEY-LEUGERS
Antique Magic

LYRA R. SAENZ
Prelude
Falsetto in the Woods: Novella
Ragtime Swing
Sonata
Song of the Sea
The Devil's Trill
Bercuese
To Heal a Songbird
Ghost March
Nocturne

PAIGE LAVOIE
I'm in Love with Mothman

ROBERT J. LEWIS
Shadow Guardian and the
Three Bears

T.S. SIMONS
Antipodes
The Liminal Space
Ouroboros
Caim
Sessrúmnir
The 45th Parallel

VALERIE WILLIS
Cedric: The Demonic Knight
Romasanta: Father of Werewolves
The Oracle: Keeper of the
Gaea's Gate
Artemis: Eye of Gaea
King Incubus: A New Reign

V.C. WILLIS
The Prince's Priest
The Priest's Assassin
The Assassin's Saint

HORROR, THRILLER, & SUSPENSE

ALAN BERKSHIRE
Jungle
Hell's Road

ERIKA LANCE
Jimmy
Illusions of Happiness
No Place for Happiness
I Hunt You

STEVE ALTIER
The Ghost Hunter

MARIA DEVIVO
Witch of the Black Circle
Witch of the Red Thorn
Witch of the Silver Locust

MARK TARRANT
The Mighty Hook
The Death Riders
Howl of the Windigo
Guts and Garter Belts

DISCOVER MORE AT
4 HORSEMENPUBLICATIONS.COM

Lightning Source UK Ltd.
Milton Keynes UK
UKHW012006240123
415916UK00016B/226/J